Wanted! A Horse!

By the same author

_____

Kristy's Courage

Babbis Friis

Wanted!
A Horse!

Translated from the Norwegian by
Lise Sømme McKinnon

Illustrated by Charles Robinson

Harcourt Brace Jovanovich, Inc., New York

Originally published in Norway by N. W. Damn & Son
under the title of *Hest På Ønskelisten*.

ISBN 0-15-294750-7
Library of Congress Catalog Card Number: 72-153952
Printed in the United States of America
First American edition
B C D E F G H I J

Wanted! A Horse!

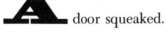 door squeaked.

There were whispers and patterings. Then came some heavier sounds, but just from a stool being moved and from somebody climbing onto it. The heavy thudding sounds, the clumping and trampling he was expecting, did not come.

Was expecting? No. Was hoping for? Maybe not even that. He knew he would have been crazy to have believed it.

Even so, he lay there, stiff as a poker, with his mouth open, hardly breathing. He just *listened.*

Now then! Steps in the hall! The linoleum with a rug on it . . . that would certainly muffle the sounds a lot. But . . . *that* much?

The door handle groaned a little, and then the door squeaked as a narrow strip of light slowly broadened.

There was the fluttering of little candle flames above the cake . . . Mother's sleepy eyes blinking in the direction of his bed . . . her smile that lifted up all the curves and hollows of her face.

"Are you really awake? Many happy returns!"

Father came shuffling behind in his long dressing gown. Father only . . . with some packages and things in his arms.

Mother placed the cake on his bedside table. Soft, warm hands stroked his cheeks and ears. He might have been three years old again.

"Svein, darling!"

Father stacked packages on the coverlet and leaned something thin and cardboard-like against the bed. He stumbled on his dressing gown belt.

"Many ahh-happy returns!"

The giant yawn made the thin face about half a yard longer. All the lines and wrinkles in it, too, for Father was made with a ruler and Mother with dividers.

Svein's hand was pumped up and down once or twice.

"And now you're surely going to look at your presents?"

"I knew it, of course. Knew it for certain." Svein was talking himself into it with all his might. "Up with the corners of your mouth," he said to himself. "Then it looks as if you're smiling. Up, up!"

He fumbled with string and sort of heard that Lena —his married sister—had knitted the patterned mittens. "And the skates—well, you see . . . we bought them from Morten at half price. But they are newly ground and should be as good as new. You'd better put some cotton wool into the toes to begin with. There is a card from Morten here, by the way. Look, with a picture of the college, Gothenburg Technical. He is certainly lucky to have gotten in there, isn't he, even if it costs plenty!"

8

"Oh yes, yes. And here is another package to be opened, Svein." Mother made it her business to see he kept his mind on the job.

A large box of water colors and brushes to liberate his imagination. Had she not gotten beyond that section yet? Mother read books about child education "for the grandchildren's sake," with grandchildren underlined. In that way she made sure Svein didn't think it had anything to do with him. So far there was only one very young grandchild.

He thanked them for both the paintbox and the hockey skates.

Father nodded, and Mother beamed with a broad smile.

"We'll talk about ski equipment when we get nearer Christmas, but"—Father cleared his throat and stretched himself—"here is your horse!"

"W-what!" Svein gave such a gasp that the flames blew flat and two candles went out.

"Yes, indeed, we're beginning to get used to this joke now, so we thought we had better give you a little of your own back."

A joke! So that's what they called it. Really. He would remember that.

A picture of a horse. A picture! A paper horse! Hah. A crashing great joke. Perhaps it, too, was in the book.

Svein had to blow out the remaining ten candles in a hurry; otherwise, he might risk killing himself laughing.

"It is an awfully good picture," was Father's opinion.

"Is that meant to be a horse? I'd better get my glasses." Mother laughed. "Well, you'll have to get up now, my dear!"

And then they went out.

It had started at the circus on the birthday he became . . . probably seven; he was in the first grade.

A row of ponies had run around and around, making the sawdust fly. When the man in the top hat cracked his whip, the little horses had stopped dead. A little brown one had stood right in front of Svein's and Lena's seats. It blinked and looked at him. Yes, it had looked straight into Svein's eyes. It neighed and tossed its head so that the forelock danced. "I should certainly like to make friends with you," it seemed to say.

Snap! The whip had cracked a hole in the air, and all the short pony legs ran-ran-ran.

After the performance was over, all those who wanted to had been allowed to ride on the ponies. All those, that is, who did not have a sister with a friend who could not wait another second for her. Lena had dragged Svein away with her. He had just had time to see that another boy was allowed to sit up on the little brown pony.

That year Svein wrote out his first list to Santa Claus for Christmas. It just read: PONEE.

"A toboggan is a more reliable conveyance," Santa Claus said, laughing in his beard when he delivered the gift to Svein. It was the last laugh to be laughed in *that* beard, for Svein tore it off Father.

Then came the time when Svein's only wish was to be run over or get a broken leg or polio, for his friend Finn started at riding school, but it was just for children needing to ride—as physiotherapy.

The riding school had ponies, not tiny ones like those at the circus, but just the right size. Svein had been allowed to come along and watch. Oh yes, he had patted Finn's pony but had not sat on it.

He wanted, wanted to be ill, but nothing happened. That is, finally something did happen—something impossible! Finn left—Finn who had lived wall to wall with Svein in the old row of houses ever since they were born; Finn who had dug in the sandpit with Svein and gone to nursery school with him, who had trained on the ski slope as well as he could with his bad leg; Finn who had eaten and slept, played and fought, and done homework and gone to the movies with Svein, always just with Svein.

He had had to move to Switzerland with his family. Switzerland! The name was like wiping off the blackboard with a sponge. Everything became quite black afterward.

"Svein, are you coming to eat? It's a quarter of!"

The blind, too, was black. Crash! He let it snap up, and the autumn sun hurt his eyes.

The sun was out. They said that meant Svein had

11

been good during the past year, at least if the fine weather lasted through the day. Hum! Most likely it wouldn't.

But just try explaining to parents that the only thing that can help against seeing everything black is to get a horse!

Pooh! Svein knocked over the picture in the rush to get into his trousers.

The paper horse! An angry thrust and it sailed right up onto the writing desk. There it hung on its edge, teetering for a second or two, before finding support against the wall behind it.

But . . . it was . . . it was a horse the likes of which he had never seen! Maybe it wasn't a horse at all.

A huge, wild, powerful challenge, it was, that came raging toward him, springing from his own fantasy and at the same time imposing itself on his dreams.

Come on—if you dare! Svein stood rooted, spellbound.

Suddenly he knew that he *would* have a horse. And he was going to manage to get hold of one himself! No more fuss and bother with parents.

A pony? What was that?

No! This is what his horse was going to be like: full-size, strong, and warm-blooded. Black as the night, with a keen eye. Dangerous maybe, but Svein would master it.

The super-horse.

As Svein left his room, he tore down the boldly written sign he had pinned to the door.

Wanted!
for Svein's twelfth birthday:
A Horse!
Never mind about hockey skates and one of
those bikes with small weels and cross-country
skis and boots and ski trowsers.
If only I get a HORSE!
Just a small one. A pony doesn't cost much.
And there *is* room for it in the shed.

"You've taken my knee socks! The new ones!"

"No, I haven't! Mine are new, too—at least there are
no holes in them!"

"These are far too small for me. You'll have to
change back!"

Wild yells in the hall. The younger sister held tight
to her socks, while the older ran around her trying
to pull them off her.

"Sigrid! Ella! Stop it! *Please*—I can't bear your
squabbling every day of the year!" Mama stood in the
doorway with a lighted cigarette, her eyebrows knit.

"Yes, but these socks are *not* mine—they are *far* too
small!"

"Maybe they have shrunk in the washing. Try to find
some others, or get slacks and ankle socks. You should
have something to cover your knees anyway."

"Baa to you, Shreddy! There, you hear, the socks are
mine . . ."

"Will you stop calling me that stupid name!"

"*Be quiet,* both of you! Otherwise, you are going to

do the dishes instead of going out. Then I might have a rest for once."

"I don't mind doing the dishes."

"There's nothin' to do outside anyway."

"Oh, well, never mind. You've gotten so pale these days. Go out and get some air—the rain has stopped. See that you make up again before bedtime. You never used to be at each other's throats like that before, did you now?"

"No, not *before*," Ella said.

There was a sudden silence in the hall. The sisters laced their shoes, buttoned their coats, and left.

Clouds of smoke swirled up to the ceiling, floated down again, and drew a veil across the hall mirror—a light gray veil. Mama's steps toward the ashtray were almost soundless on the sitting room carpet.

Outside there was not merely a gray veil. A fog dimmed the whole street between the high apartment houses. It was difficult to see where one house ended and the next began.

"It doesn't even smell properly of outside when we are out. It smells like a gas station." Ella poked her nose up in the air and sniffed her disapproval.

"The exhaust from the cars can't get away because of the fog. Just wait till winter comes. Our needlework teacher says that the air gets real thick with oil and fumes then—thick and greasy."

"Is that what your needlework teacher is?"

"Silly kid!" Sigrid strode along irritably. The kid, taken aback, came tripping after her.

A car splattered right through a large puddle by the edge of the sidewalk. The mud squirted onto new and old socks, although their owners jumped aside as best they could.

"What a pig! They're such rough drivers here!"

"You might as well have called him a bull. Do you remember how the bull at Bye used to tear up mud and earth when he came down by the swamp beside the spring?"

Tramp, tramp—no answer.

"Couldn't we go back now, Sigrid. It's cold."

"Can't you come along as far as the newspaper stand? That's where they all are."

"Just those awful big boys. You're crazy about boys."

"I am *not!* There's sure to be girls there, too—maybe some of the girls from your class."

"Pooh! Them!"

The soles of Ella's shoes dragged more and more slowly.

"There you are, look."

Two groups were there by the stand. In the first group, sure enough, were only bigger boys. They stood with their heads together over something in the middle, some sort of motorbike, no doubt.

"Y'r lyin'. It's done a lot more. This tire's worn right through. Y've pushed back the speedometer anyway. Y'll get no more'n a hundred and seventy-five anywhere for that."

There were high-pitched voices, deep voices, and some hoarse ones half broken.

The ginger one standing farthest out had caught sight of Sigrid.

"My! G'd ev'nin', ma'am!"

He made a low, teasing bow and let the sisters pass while he murmured something that made Sigrid's cheeks turn scarlet.

"What did he say? What was it he said?" Ella kept at her.

"Nothing, silly."

Sigrid did not see anybody she knew in the other group, although those would-be movie stars standing around there were about her own age—or a little older, maybe.

All of them were smoking, but not with quick, hungry puffs like Mama. All their movements were slow and sexy, as if a camera were following them the whole time.

Sigrid was examined out of the corner of half-closed eyes—none of them bothered to turn her head. To judge from their expressions, you would think she were a bluebottle that just happened to be flying past them —fortunately. Ella was not even a mosquito—she did not exist.

But suddenly the gang leaped into life. Two boys came zooming on a scooter and braked so suddenly that the tires and the girls shrieked in competition.

"So y' got money for gas t'day. Congratulations!"

"Money! Phooey! Y' shoulda seen the look on the guy we tapped when he spotted his tank was empty!"

Sigrid and Ella moved out of earshot.

17

"Maybe we had better go home, after all, and help Mama dry the dishes."

"Wait! Over *there* somebody's coming that I know. Slightly, anyway."

Ella lit up in an expectant smile while three girls approached.

". . . but I *refused* to wear that horrible coat. And at *last* they gave in and I got this one."

The other two admired and envied it and felt the fur around the collar. None of them noticed that they passed two girls, nor that the younger of them nodded a little hesitatingly and whispered hello.

So the pair of them turned and trudged back, only this time on the other side of the street.

"Do you think Queenie has had her calf by now, Sigrid?"

"Dunno. No. She wasn't due to calve till nearer Christmas. We'll surely have a letter about it."

"Are we going to stay here for Christmas, too? Are we not going home for visits or anything?"

Ella's voice was so tiny and unhappy. But Sigrid got furious instead of feeling sorry for her.

"This is home now. Can't you ever stop that moaning of yours! Do you think it's all that much fun for *me*? When things were going so well with Paul and everything— Look out!"

Too late!

A car . . . a swerve . . . brakes . . . a toot . . . a front fender . . . "Ella-h!!"

Tipped up . . . rolled around . . . thrown down.

Now she was lying there at Sigrid's feet—a little bundle . . . quite still.

"No!" Sigrid sobbed. "No!"

She ought to have knelt down . . . turned Ella over . . . seen if she was alive. But her body just stood there . . . couldn't be used for anything.

She heard car doors open, sensed that somebody got out, but her eyes didn't move from—

There! The bundle moved!

Ella grunted. She did not cry, but grunted like a baby pig.

A lady did what Sigrid had not managed to. She was already sitting on the asphalt and had lifted up Ella's head.

"Oof, how wet I am," said the head.

"Can—canyoumovewheredoesithurt?" The lady was not breathing either.

"I am *wet!* I fell in this mud." Ella had risen without help and pointed at her clothes to make the lady understand.

She herself did not seem to realize that she had been knocked down.

The lady, very young—almost a girl—had remained sitting in the street. Now she got to her feet, reached out her arms, and felt down the whole of Ella.

"Are you *sure* it doesn't hurt anywhere?"

She brushed and patted the little girl, who wriggled and looked shyly sideways at the boy—for there was a boy, too.

"She walked into the crosswalk so suddenly, and I

didn't see you two in the fog beforehand. But I wasn't driving fast, was I, Svein?"

"Oh, no. You had your directional blinking and tooted—"

"It was my fault," Sigrid began. "I should have looked after . . ." "Shouldn't just have walked there making all that fuss and forgetting about the traffic," she thought to herself.

The young lady, however, waved aside whatever she was going to say next. "Jump in and I'll drive you home."

Several cars had slowed down, and the gang from the stand came drifting along to gape.

The sisters were only too glad when the car doors banged shut and hid them.

"Wouldn't the best thing be to call on a doctor or go to a first-aid station?" Worried dark blue eyes could be seen in the car mirror.

The protest from the back seat deafened all ears. "No! That would *not* be the best thing."

"Sounds more as if that would be the worst," the boy said with a laugh, and glanced over his shoulder toward Ella.

The lady, too, smiled. "Well, well. Then you'd better tell me where you live and your names. I am Lena Holm, and Svein is my brother."

While Sigrid was telling their names and address, she took a peep at the two in the front seat.

This Svein wasn't much like his sister. She had soft,

gentle features and fair silky curls against the neck of her sweater.

His profile was the kind that Sigrid liked to draw, with forehead, nose, and chin well out, and real deep dents in between. His jaw looked a bit stubborn, though, and the tuft of hair over his forehead reminded her strongly of the bristles on their old sow. Not much silk there.

"My knee is hurting me now," Ella whispered, "but don't say anything." She sat with her hand shielding a skinned place. Sigrid searched for a handkerchief.

"Have you lived long here in this street?" Lena wanted to know. She was just turning in among the apartment houses.

"Only a month and a half. We didn't get here till August."

"We've never lived in town before! But Mama has . . . she comes from here. That's why . . . "

Ella received a nudge in her side to prevent her from making a slip of the tongue.

"Have you made many friends here?"

As Sigrid did not say anything, Ella had to answer once more.

"Oh, no. Nobody needs any more friends. They all seem to have plenty of them already."

After that no more was said till they arrived.

"I am *so* glad this turned out all right," Lena said with a sigh, while she helped—almost carried—Ella out. "Now that I see how easy it is to run over somebody, I'll hardly dare to use my husband's car any more. And how I shall ever dare to let my own little girl out alone, I don't know. She is only six months old now, so I'm glad there'll be a while yet. So long. Good luck! We'll be seeing you again!"

It was lucky that Mama had drawn the kitchen curtains. No point in telling her about this.

Ella was wiped and tidied up a bit before they went in and did not look particularly run over.

The sisters were, on the whole, well satisfied with their outing. Something had happened, at least, even if one girl's knee was hurting and the other's conscience was a little tender, too.

"Svein dear," came a chirrup from upstairs when he returned from school. "Lena wondered if you would do her a favor and deliver some books for her today." Mother was standing in the upstairs hallway, wearing a flowered apron and ironing clothes.

"Books?"

"Yes, she looked in this morning with Mette and got out some of her books from the box in the attic."

Mother's voice was so easy and bright that it smelled child-education book a mile off.

"Where are the books going, then?"

"Surely it says on the parcel. Wait a moment and I'll find it." The head vanished behind the ironing board up there.

Svein shot into the sitting room. He had to find out

at which paragraph the bookmark was now. The horrible bookmark he had painted on cardboard with his birthday paints.

The book was on the shelf below the radio table as usual. The mark had been moved from "Stimulate the Imagination" back to the beginning of "Difficulties in Making Contact."

Svein leafed quickly through the chapter. "Activizing Reticent Children"—"Hobby Clubs"—"Music Groups." Just the thing for Lena's Mette-baby, this. It *was*, after all, intended for bringing up grandchildren, wasn't it? Pooh!

"Keep an Open Door"—"Ask the Friends Home." He really had been left in no doubt that this chapter had been read.

Mother came to the head of the stairs again. "This is the parcel, dear."

To Ella and Sigrid Tyrgrend!

Oh, so that was it! Light began to dawn. Those two also had "difficulty in making contact," and Svein was always by himself, Mother complained.

Hocus-pocus! So Lena and Mother had concocted a magic brew. The three of them were to become friends!

In this house people were world champions at inventing rotten schemes!

No matter how gruff he made himself or how loudly he protested, however, Mother managed to twist him the way she wanted today. Odd.

Well bribed with four slices of sweet wheat bread—

thickly spread with honey—and having avoided as many embraces from the plump rosy apron, he was ready to set off.

But he did manage to get back a little. Before he left, he called up to the ironing board.

"Don't expect me for dinner. I'm taking a trip out to the racecourse first!"

A slightly tousled mop of gray hair and two eyes as round as marbles showed above the edge of the ironing board.

"Race" was all she had time to say before he banged the door shut.

Served them right to get something to chew over. They had just about thought of *everything* to "activize" him—everything except what he wanted. How far did they think they could go?

After all, he did not like to draw and paint, nor did he like to model. He couldn't manage to make it look like anything, got angry, scribbled, bungled, and slapped the lumps of clay together.

"Well now, for all *I* know, they may be works of art," Mother said, and kept every bit of it. Really!

The recorder they shoved at him last spring was more of a success. With it he managed to make so many heart-rending squeals during the afternoon rest hour that Father suggested they might shelve the recorder for some time, "till Svein becomes slightly more musical."

It then became a matter of getting him out of doors. Engage in sport! Take your children out into nature!

Mother had rheumatism and had trouble enough getting up and down the stairs.

And it certainly wasn't much fun going for a Sunday walk along the roads with Father. Father, as straight as a poker, togged out in his ancient sports suit, hat, and walking stick, while other fathers and sons jogged into the woods in track suits. True, in the mornings Father performed knee bends in the sitting room, making the whole house creak, but so far he had not become noticeably younger or more athletic because of them.

"There must be somebody in your class you can go hiking with?"

Sure. Many of his classmates were OK. Only it didn't work out. They were tied up in their own interests and had their own friends, and what's more they lived so far away.

Then there were some who were *not* so right, both in school and outside. Rolly, for example. He came forward with ideas all the time. Svein could have a playmate there, you bet. Only Mother and Father might get just a little bit of a shock if they had an inkling of what those boys were up to in their spare time.

But it must surely soon seep into their heads that they ought to leave Svein in peace! True enough, he had taken it somewhat easy since Finn left, hadn't bothered to start anything. But *now!*

It had now been agreed by himself and the superhorse on the wall that he would become a horseowner. And, as he had said to Mother, he was going to take the bus right out to the racecourse that very day. He was sure to find somebody to talk to there who could give him a hint about prices. Not just what the horse would cost, but also how much was needed to keep it. Once he had that information, he could begin to make plans.

Only he had first to get rid of the parcel for these pesky girls. Fortunately, a card went with it, so he did not need to say much. Just bow, hand it over, and say bye-bye.

Hooray, he didn't even have to do that, as nobody was home. Perhaps he didn't ring very hard or very long, but the bell had at least given a ping.

The parcel of books was too thick to go through the letter slot, so he simply put it down in the corner by the door with the name "Tyrgrend" on it.

"In the corner by the door marked Tyrgrend," he hummed gaily, jumping feet together down the stairs. Tomorrow he would have forgotten the difficult name. No need to remember it either, tra-la-la.

There was a sickly sweet smell of concrete in the stairway. New apartment houses these. All modern surely, with oil heating and things. No carrying coke from cold cellars as others had to.

Served Mother and Lena right, this—that the girls were not at home. Therefore, no romance could come out of it.

Nice weather outside. Temperature about right. Life was tolerable on the whole.

The patches of the hill that were visible between the

roofs as he walked along the street were like pieces in a jigsaw puzzle of a brilliant autumn painting. Looking at nice colors was just fine, so long as he didn't have to paint them.

Ten minutes till the bus was due. A couple of hours, at least, would pass before he would be back home—the racecourse was not particularly close to town.

Blast, drat, and worse than that. There those girls were coming—or was it them? Yes, it really was.

The tall one was just taking the little one by the hand while they crossed the street—she seemed to have learned that much anyway.

An iron post with a stop sign—not much for hiding behind. But could he possibly turn and pretend . . . oh, no.

"Hi! Svein!" It was the smaller one calling, Ella. Svein remembered clearly the soft thud when the bumper hit her.

So he had to turn his head, then, slowly, look very surprised, and say, "Oh, hi! It's you!"

They both nodded and came nearer.

Some fine broomstick this Sigrid was. Why must all girls be so idiotically tall? She wasn't too bad-looking right up on top. Now she flung her long dark hair over her shoulders and smiled at him.

"Are you waiting for the bus?"

"Yes, but I've been up delivering a parcel at your place. It's lying outside the door."

"A parcel? For *us?*"

"Not from *me!*" Now they probably thought . . . in a great rush Svein burbled out that they were Lena's books. "She's my sister. And they aren't new. And there's a card from her inside."

Those two didn't look in any way put out because of that.

"What books are they?" Ella looked up at him excitedly with brown eyes from under a lock of brown hair. The whole girl, small and sturdy, with strong teeth, reminded him of something. But what?

Svein said he had no idea what books were in the parcel. "Probably some she thinks you might like to read."

The girls had his permission to go home now.

Would this awful bus never come?

"What school do you go to?" Sigrid flung her hair once more.

"To Vold."

"Oh. We have to go all the way to Marton's. There was no room for us any nearer."

"We go on the streetcar *every* day!" Ella did not seem sorry about that anyway. Perhaps they had never seen streetcars before they came to town.

"What grade are you in?"

"Sixth." They'd better stop these questions soon.

"You're right between us, then," Ella said, laughing. "But I guess I'm likely to flunk because the way they teach here is so different."

"Mmm. Isn't that the top of a bus there, behind that truck?"

"Where?" Both girls turned, but they found something else to look at.

All three became so absorbed in it that the bus drove up, stopped, and started again without anybody's having boarded it.

From the side street came a clop-clop-clop, and into the crossing came not just one horse, but a whole lot! A string of horses, with riders bobbing on their backs! Here, in the middle of the traffic, among cars, streetcars, and blocks of houses, the whole thing looked weird—as weird for those country girls as for the town boy.

"Brona!" Ella suddenly shouted. "It's Brona, Sigrid. D'y think it's Brona?"

"Nope! Brona has a much larger blaze. But this one . . . " Sigrid pointed. She, too, was excited now. "He's the spittin' image of one of the horses at Rud!" Suddenly she covered her mouth and turned very red above it.

Svein had not noticed the way they had talked, though. He compared the horses to the one in the picture at home. None of them came up to it, of course. But among the big heavy ones and the smaller but still very sturdy ones, some more slender horses stood out —obvious thoroughbreds. Their hoofs hardly touched the asphalt, they tap-tapped their way so lightly and softly. The riders held them on tight reins, making the strong necks bend.

Oh, yes, the riders! They were mainly young people. Most of them were boys and girls a little older than

Svein, but he did see some fellows of his own age. He called up to the last of them, "Where are all these horses going?"

"Up to the winter stables at Ligård."

"Whereabouts at Ligård?"

The boy raised his arm and explained something, but it was lost in the trampling and clattering.

At the other side of the crossing, the group got up speed and were soon out of sight.

The car drivers, who had been waiting considerately, shifted and drove off. In the street everything was back to normal once more.

No, not everything. Sigrid and Ella stood looking after the horses. But how different they were!

Tall, thin, pale Sigrid now had roses in her cheeks, as red as those on Mother's apron. And her eyes—they had grown at least double in size!

Ella, the little tub, trotted along to see as far as possible around the corner. Then her sister's hand held her back, but even so she was one big smile.

"We'll follow! Come on, Sigrid. We'll go with them to the stables!"

"But do you think we *can?*" She didn't say, "We can't." The sisters looked at each other, then at Svein.

"Do you know where Ligård is?"

"Sure. It's not far by streetcar. We could walk, too, of course, but they're so far on ahead . . . "

Whyever did he say this? Everything was one muddle in his head: the racecourse, these horses, Ligård, the girls.

Oh, well, the bus to the racecourse had gone. After all, why couldn't he ask the price of one of these horses? The road to Ligård was shorter, too. But then there were the girls. He would have them to drag along in that case.

"We'll do it then! We'll take the streetcar. Maybe we'll arrive first. And maybe I'll get to pat the mare that is so like Brona!"

"Mama won't be home for an hour yet. Can we manage to be back by then?" Sigrid had turned to Svein and looked as if she were consulting a grownup.

"Yes—it should be possible." Svein straightened a little, feeling proud because he knew more than they did.

"Let's go, then. First to the trolley stop!" But once more the sister-arm caught Ella up. "So you have money for the streetcar, have you?"

Oh, golly. Svein had *forgotten* money! So he couldn't have gotten to the racecourse, no matter how much he wanted to. He pretended to search through his pockets, but he knew perfectly well that his wallet was lying in the drawer at home.

"We'll run along to our place and get some! I'm sure I've got enough for all of us."

Maybe this girl Sigrid was all right after all. Quite pretty, too, really. And Ella! What was it she looked like when she ran like that with a tuft of hair up on end?

The pony! The little brown one at the circus. *That's* what she was like!

There was louder thunder on the stairway when those three stormed up the stairs than there had been in the street when sixteen horses had cantered along it.

At Ligård station Svein went over to the lady at the newsstand and asked if she had seen some riders pass.

"Gunder's horses? Certainly. They have come home for the winter—it's so nice to have them here again. Don't you know where they stay? It's on the main farm at Ligård itself—in the stables there."

The lady pointed out where he should go, but Sigrid and Ella were far ahead already.

"Hi!" Svein was panting when he overtook them. "How did you know that this was the right road?"

"We played Nancy Drew, of course!" Both of them laughed and nodded toward a heap of steaming fresh horse manure.

"Oh. Elementary, that is."

"What does that mean?"

Sherlock Holmes had worked up such speed that he did not seem to hear Ella's question.

But Sigrid knew the answer. "Something that is so easy that beginners can manage it!"

It was likewise elementary to find the way to the stables when they entered the main farmyard.

Trampling and shouts, clatter and rattling, snorts and neighs—all streamed out from an open door on the whitewashed ground floor of the barn building.

"Oh boy, this is a huge one!" Ella was wondering how many horses the barn would hold, but she was hushed by her sister.

They stood by the door and peered into the long stable.

"Must be room for at least a hundred horses!" Sigrid craned her neck while Ella slipped inside.

"*Feel* this lovely smell!" Her small face wrinkled up in delight while she closed her eyes and breathed in the rich smells that wafted toward the door.

Svein's nose also wrinkled itself, but not exactly in pleasure.

"Get out of the way there!" They were chased back out by a biggish boy who was leading a horse behind him. "We can't have children in the stable now. Not *ladies* either," he added with a grin, for Sigrid had tossed her head indignantly so her hair danced.

He shut the lower part of the Dutch door and bolted it. Then they could stand and peep over the edge.

Boys and girls in dungarees and pullovers unsaddled horses, tethered and pushed them into their stalls. Horses' heads and rumps, harnesses and buckets were all along the center aisle.

Some trouble arose in the far corner. There were whinnies and kicks at walls, and in between they could see a black horse's head rising toward the ceiling.

"Gunder! You must come and lend a hand with Pronto," somebody called. "He won't go in here!"

By and by calm descended, but then came new shouts for Gunder.

"Where's Farouk going?" "This halter rope won't hold, Gunder!" "Gunder! Tuba's leg is worse."

Out of the confusion came a voice, unruffled, calm. Everybody got an answer and everything was put in order in due course.

At first they saw only his back among the horse stalls. Not a broad back—the shoulders sticking out from the worn leather vest were on the narrow side. His waist was as slim as a young boy's. His legs were short, and if they were not exactly like a wheel, at least a baby pig could easily have run between Gunder's riding-breeched knees!

Then, lugging a heavy sack, he turned so that the light fell on his face.

Oh, sure enough. Small or not—this was the boss: you could tell that from far off.

The strong gray eyes swept over the stable to see if all was going as it should. His hair was thick and gray-ish black, with a snowy-white streak on the right-hand side. But below the hair he looked very untidy—as if he had been out a lot in a strong crosswind. His nose was twisted and bent, and his mouth was also on a slant.

Now he grimaced against the sun and looked even more on the bias. He nodded his head ever so slightly toward those three in the doorway. "Hi."

Nod, nod, nod from the spectators.

"You'll have to wait till another day to come inside, I'm afraid." Soft country voice, but it was obeyed!

Gunder turned inward again. "Kalle, you can open

35

this sack for me. And see if you can find a couple more buckets."

Presto! Kalle appeared on the spot, slit open a sack, and dashed on.

The three spectators retreated reluctantly but bumped into somebody—into many! Without their having noticed, a whole lot of other children had come into the yard and had crowded together in back of them.

Their space in the doorway was rapidly filled, and heads at all levels were stretched to get a glimpse of what was going on inside.

"Oh, see how Sokka is carrying on! She doesn't like this stable. My, how Rosemary's foal has grown during the summer! He's almost fully grown."

The children from the neighborhood knew all the horses and most of the riders. But they were not let inside the door either.

"Gunder is very strict. He won't let anybody take care of the horses before he's sure they are not up to any nonsense."

"Oh, yes. Kalle in there—he had to wait ages before he was allowed to do more than just sweep the stable."

"Kalle was a pretty wild guy, too, in the old days!"

Sigrid and Ella pricked up their ears while they wandered around a little outside the group. Svein strolled over to some younger boys.

"What does Gunder keep all these horses for?"

The boys answered on top of one another. "He hires them out, of course, to people wanting to ride. On Sundays it's crowded here. And then he runs long trips in the summer. In the winter it's sleigh rides. Some horses he has on livery, too."

"Where have they been now, before they came up here?"

"At the Point—there was a summer camp. Wish I could have been in on it." One of the boys sighed.

"Pooh, gotta be a millionaire for that," one of the others snorted.

"Anybody know what these horses cost?"

"Cost—to buy you mean?" Nobody knew that.

"Is it expensive to hire one, then?"

"Dunno how much Gunder wants now."

"Five dollars an hour. Far too much," someone else said.

"You get a good cut rate if you shovel a ton of muck first. But this boy doesn't. It's only the meatheads in there who do that sort of thing."

Where on earth had Rolly come from, Svein wondered. Suddenly he was strutting around here, as if he owned the whole yard. He inspected some saddles that were lying outside along the stable wall.

But when the white streak in Gunder's hair turned up among the heads in the doorway—then Rolly had just as suddenly disappeared.

"Get cracking! Move!" the horse on the wall said. "If you are going to take part in a ride like that one, you have to start training at once!"

Yes, yes. Sure, that's what Svein wanted to do. But how? There were lots of things to be figured out.

That he was going to buy a horse was certain. The moment and the funds—more uncertain.

He had one hundred dollars in his bankbook that Grandfather had given him for his christening. The sum in the school bank account had grown to thirty dollars. But would he be allowed to withdraw all that?

If he was to start riding at once, he had to hire a horse. Then he would have to use the money he was saving to buy it. Oh, how difficult!

Ligård was lying there like a magnet, pulling—pulling—pulling. And the super-horse chased him along, forced him, and threatened him.

Altogether, the effect was so powerful that he wasn't quite sure where he was or where he was going, nor what he said.

"Svein, what is the name of the king who ruled in Sweden at that time?" It was the history teacher asking.

"Gunder," he received for an answer.

"Svein dear, where's the shirt that needs washing?" Mother called from the bathroom.

"In the stable," was the information *she* got.

No, there was nothing for it but to go up to Ligård. Maybe he could straighten out his plans once he had talked to Gunder.

This time Svein looked at the farm carefully. He did not walk up the main drive, which was probably only used by the people living in the large white house with the pillars in front. There was an orchard—wasn't it called an arbor?

The farm buildings lay so far behind it that it was quicker to follow the tractor track past the fields. The barn with the stables and cowbarn, the farm manager's house, the greenhouse, the store house, and some other little buildings were lying in a spacious quadrangle around the yard. It was not quite a quadrangle, though, because toward the main building grew a hedge, which divided the trampled grassy slope in the outer farmyard from the gravel, the rosebeds, and the ornamental shrubs in the inner yard.

Svein thought he saw the owner's hat above the hedge, but it turned out to be a signpost with arrows pointing to various offices in the main building.

So, no one lived in the house—there were just offices there. Pity!

Svein shuffled in straw and dust along the tractor track toward the stable. Does one knock on a stable door?

To be on the safe side, he did, but felt somewhat silly. Nobody answered, either horse or man. The big outer door was unlocked, and the Dutch door inside it was open.

Oof! Ella's "lovely" smell almost knocked him out. She must have meant it in fun.

There was no longer any chaos down the center aisle. The stable was not nearly so full, several of the stalls being empty. The innermost one, too, where there had been such trouble the last time—it looked as if they were building something there. Planks and tools were scattered around.

When he entered, there was not much disturbance. The large black, the little dun, the medium-brown animals scarcely moved. A horse shook its mane so that rings and straps rattled. Another took some small steps backward, while a third turned its head and looked at Svein. Then it snorted heavily and resignedly. It sounded like "Ah, well."

Svein hadn't exactly expected them to flip their tails and neigh a welcome to him, of course.

But . . . what was this? Kssjt! Suddenly he was standing inside a bale of hay! Then it went kssjt again, and some more fell down on top of him.

"Hey! Wait." He fought himself free, jumped aside, and peered up.

"Somebody there?" Gunder's voice.

A few yellow straws were stuck in the gray-black hair. They worked loose and sailed down when the twisted nose appeared in the hatch in the ceiling.

"It's you, is it?" It didn't look as if Gunder was much surprised.

"Yes. It is . . . it is Svein Moen. I was here the day before yesterday—when you arrived."

"So I saw."

Imagine being able to remember that after having shot only a glance at the gang hanging about the doorway!

Gunder gathered in more hay with the hayfork before he leaned his head forward once more.

"Look out there!" A new load fell on the floor beside Svein.

He thought of the super-horse, braced himself, and asked, "Are—are any of the horses here for sale?"

"Oh, no. No, they aren't exactly." The answer came from above, but the hatch was empty again.

"How much, roughly, do they cost, the ones you have here?"

"Are you thinking of buying a horse?" Now the gray eyes were fixed directly upon Svein. It almost felt as if he had a pair of car headlights on him.

He nodded.

Then one boot, followed by another, came down through the hatch, and, hepp, there was Gunder hanging by his arms and letting himself drop with a supple spring.

Very strong he was! But surely he had gone up by some other way.

"You'd better tell me a little about it, then."

Tell! Explain things one could only feel inside oneself—things one *must* have and *must* do.

In addition, Gunder came out with questions in the middle of the "story."

"Have you ridden much?"

He had to answer no, of course. After that everything gummed up for him.

Gunder carried big armfuls of hay to the stalls while Svein stood there stuttering.

Then came a brief halt to the feeding. Those horses that had received their hay were contentedly munch-

ing and chewing, while the rest were stamping rest-
lessly, nibbling at their tethers and stretching their
necks after Gunder.

Gunder chewed, too—the words. He—mm—scarcely
thought they were fine enough for Svein's use, those
horses he had stabled here. And the price—mmm—
well, if he really wanted a fine horse, thoroughbred
without any kind of defect, then he must surely go up
to . . .

"Hm. Between nine and fifteen hundred somewhere."

Ugh, how humiliating! Svein had seen it on Gunder
—knew the answer before it came. It was obvious that
a thoroughbred would cost more than a *hundred* and
some dollars! Now he had made a perfect idiot of himself.

"If you want to win races with it, you'll have to go to
several thousand. But, of course, you can get a usable
horse for some two or three hundred as well."

"I see! Well, I'll have to think about it."

"Oh, yes. There's maybe not all that much of a
hurry."

Gunder swept together another armful of hay and
stamped off. Svein began to draw toward the door.

"And you aren't interested in any riding, sort of in
the meantime, before you're going to buy?"

"Interested. Sure!" Svein almost shouted. "But—five
dollars an hour . . . "

Well, it all depended. For those giving a hand with
the horses and helping in the stables, it wasn't more

than three. Some of the boys worked so much that they didn't pay at all.

"Is that possible?"

Yes, but *they* had been around here for many years, so they were experienced horsemen.

"It really takes more than *one* day to become that. But it's just as sure that one day has to be the first one."

Svein was none the wiser for these deep thoughts.

"Thank you for . . . " For what? "I had better go now."

He could thank Gunder for the information, maybe.

"You'll have to try and talk nicely to your father, son. And then we'll probably see you up here some other day, too."

Gunder should know how impossible it was to talk "nicely" to Father.

"Riding lessons! How well off do you think we are! Anyway, this point has been raised before."

Sure, thank you, so Svein remembered.

"But this is not the Riding Club! It's at a farm, and it costs only three dollars an hour!"

"Only! Do you know what we have to pay out every month for Morten? And you will also need further education of some kind. And housing and food and clothes and all the prices that have gone up and the taxes . . . " In short, the whole rigmarole. And more, too.

"It is not just payment for lessons. There's also expensive equipment, boots, riding breeches, and all that. No, we are willing to go far for your sake, my boy, but there *are* limits. Young people nowadays don't seem to think so."

He took that one, too.

The result was the usual. When anger seized him, Svein grew blazing hot inside. The heat rushed right up into his head. First it boiled; then it turned to a crust. Then he couldn't talk.

So, he did not say that he had intended to earn some of the riding money himself. Babysit for Lena, do errands for Mother, rake leaves off the lawn—such things as he always gotten a little for doing. After all, he *wanted* to manage on his own.

"Moreover"—Father could not be stopped—"moreover, I don't think it is right to use money on such things when so many children in the world are starving and suffering. Just look!" He slapped the newspaper and held it up for Svein to see the starvation headlines.

"Would you take that money and send it to hungry children instead then?" Svein suddenly saw a chance of driving Father into a corner.

"You must not turn things upside down, now, Svein. We are, after all, not talking about money we *have*. This money we do *not* have, and for that reason it obviously cannot be used for anything."

Oh, no. It was no use, *never* any use.

Mother had had baby Mette all afternoon, and just before dinner Lena came.

"Everything been all right here?"

"Yes, indeed. Mette and I have had a really lovely time!" Mother was nice as pie and held forth about everything the grandchild had been up to. "Oh, they really should never grow older than six months."

"You don't say," Lena remarked, with a chuckle.

"Oof, yes. This book, you know, you can have it, Lena. I think it's better to read it while the children are small. Later on it doesn't seem to be any use." The last words were followed by a deep sigh, and Mother nodded up in the direction of Svein's room.

"Is it bad again? I thought he seemed surprisingly alert and nice the last time he came to see us."

"Yes, yes. He did seem to have pulled himself together for a while, and we thought he had gotten over it. But *now* it's worse than ever. Doesn't utter a word all day. Won't budge outside in the afternoons and evenings. Just sits and gapes at that horse picture every time I peep in."

After dinner Lena commanded Svein to dry the dishes while Mother and Father had a rest in the sitting room. The porta-crib with Mette was standing on two chairs alongside the kitchen table.

"It's time you stopped that moping, Svein. You'll

have to get some other friends. Finn isn't the only person in the world, surely."

"It isn't *that*."

"But you must have grown out of that horse nonsense by now. You can't be so childish that you think you can keep a horse *here!*"

"Oh no, but . . . "

"Mother and Father do their very best to make you happy—"

"Only they do the wrong things."

"Uhrr-rrr," came from the cot. Mette smiled and lifted her doll-size hands toward Svein.

But Lena blew up, as quickly and powerfully as Svein himself.

"You are a spoiled blob of an afterthought—that's what you are!" She said more, too, and Svein let her carry on. He dried dinner plates and shut up.

It was strange with Lena—she could say quite a lot without making him angry. Little by little the scolding died down—she just glared angrily into the greasy water and splashed a bit more than was necessary.

Then Svein told about Ligård and Gunder and what Father had said.

Svein was sitting upstairs with his homework when Lena prepared the coffee tray and marched to the sitting room with it. Her parents were gradually waking up while she put out the cups.

"As far as I can understand from what I've seen in this book, Mother, riding should be right on target."

"What target, dear?" Mother smoothed her hair and

the divan cushion and yawned politely behind her hand.

"Well, it does say that children should be encouraged to go in for activities creating contact—for hobbies that will bring them together with other young people!" Lena dramatically hit out with the napkin.

"Don't come here and tell me we haven't tried *that*." Then Mother sat hunched up, her eyes fixed on the coffee tray. "My goodness! Haven't I read it somewhere else, too! All about what a fine atmosphere is created in company with animals and. . . . How could I possibly have failed to get the message from this eternal horse talk. It goes to show you!"

Mrs. Moen more or less shot up from the divan and over to the easy chair. There the evening edition of the newspaper was brutally torn off the slumbering face.

Father grunted and blinked, bewildered at two women in fighting mood.

It was on a Monday they had been at Ligård for the first time.

Tuesday after school Ella said, "Surely we can go to the stable today, Sigrid? They won't be so busy now."

"We should wait a little," Sigrid suggested. "Obviously they have a lot to do the next day as well. We mustn't make him fed up with our fuss."

Wednesday Ella said, "Today he won't get fed up with our fuss, for now we haven't been there since the day before yesterday. Come on, let's go!"

"We won't get in, only two girls. It's much better if we are along with a boy. Maybe Svein will come over here today. We'll wait and see."

Thursday Ella said, "*Today* . . . "

"We'll pop over to where Svein lives," Sigrid went on. "He's sure to be outside there somewhere. And then we'll ask if he wants to come."

They had passed his row of houses on the way down from Ligård, so they knew the way. But the sisters trudged back and forth in front of the row of old concrete houses a long time. They went around the block and returned and peered into the little yards with thick hedges on the sides, but they did not see Svein.

"We can go over and ring the bell, can't we!"

"But, Ella!" The sisterly arm held her back. "We can't go and *ask* for a boy."

Friday Ella said nothing after school, for then she had vanished.

"Maybe she has made friends with a classmate at last," Sigrid thought. "Gone home with her, or something. Lucky duck!"

The days she and Ella finished at the same time they always waited for each other and took the same streetcar. Today Ella had only had three classes. But at least she could have left a message for Sigrid at home.

Sigrid strolled out to look for her. She didn't quite like this. Now, where could they possibly live, the girls in Ella's class?

Oddly enough, Sigrid's legs must have thought that Ella's friends lived in the same street, in the same row of houses, as Svein, for that is where they had taken her before Sigrid had had time to think.

This time Svein was there. He was raking leaves on the little lawn in front of the house.

Sigrid stopped short as if she had quite suddenly caught sight of him. She called his name.

Svein turned, mumbled hello, but didn't smile.

"You haven't seen Ella anywhere, have you?"

"Ella? No."

"She isn't home."

"Oh."

He was shy, Sigrid thought. How sweet! Mighty shy now that only the two of them were there. She smiled warmly and soothingly, flung her hair over her shoulders, and said, "I suppose I'd better go on searching."

Then they said, "See you," and Svein continued the raking.

It did not matter that he was a year younger or that he was shorter than Sigrid. He might soon enough grow tall.

Sigrid walked homeward with measured steps. The march she hummed within herself sounded: "I love him, I love him, I love, love him."

"But you have to *find* Ella!"

Mama could certainly go pale—as light beige as the duster coat she had just started unbuttoning.

Her eyes, hair, and the brown leather buttons were

the only things about her that had any color. They were all the same color, come to think of it.

"Something might have *happened!*"

In a flash Sigrid again saw Ella tossed in the air and thrown down in front of the car wheels.

"I *shall* find her." The older sister ran out, red and shamefaced.

It took a long time. The sun had almost set in red clouds and Sigrid was almost right up by Ligård station when a little figure in slacks and a yellow sweater came running down the hill.

Her face was one big delighted grin that didn't change in the slightest, even though Sigrid scolded her and asked if she was quite mad.

"I sneaked inside." Ella chortled. "Two big boys were cleaning out the stables when I arrived. They chased me, but later on they went out for a smoke. Then I crept in without their noticing! I got around to say hello to them all, except the black stallion, who was angry and kicked. But then the boys came back in and threw me out." Ella giggled. "But they laughed almost. They weren't really mad."

There was no point in saying anything at all to Ella now. She had been bitten by the stable bug.

Saturday evening was almost wholly nice.

Mama had the day off from work, and so everything was clean and tidy.

The supper table was to be a surprise, so they

51

weren't allowed into the room before it was set—with red maple leaves and crab in a dish!

"There was a crab sale in town, and I couldn't resist these. Will you have lemonade or apple juice? Aha, one of each, just as I thought. I'll chalk it up if you ever happen both to choose the same."

Ella just talked about the horses at Ligård. "There was a colt there! A yearling. He was such a beauty! Crazy mad!"

"What's the great big attraction up there at that stable?" asked Mama, clicking at the tip of Ella's nose with a crab claw. "Surely the two of you have seen enough horses in your day!"

"It feels almost like *home* when we're up there."

Mama carefully replaced the claw on the dish, and Sigrid busied herself picking out meat from the thin legs on her plate.

Things were stirring on Ligård farm on Sunday!

Some horses were having trial runs with their riders. Others were being saddled in front of the stables, and one was being led to the drinking trough.

Young and old, men and women of all ages and with all sorts of sports clothes milled around with heavy saddles or talked kindly with their animal friends, patting them and giving them lumps of sugar.

"There you see, Father?" Svein nodded. "You don't need expensive clothes. It's fine with jeans and rubber boots."

"Just look at *that!*" Father's walking stick swung over to point at an elegant pair in riding costume, with spurs, hunt cap, and crop, who were just drawing in their reins, ready to start.

"Those there aren't Gunder's horses. He just looks after them. It must be the owners themselves who are riding them."

Svein looked enviously at the stable lads who ran around tightening girths, lifting children onto horses' backs, and getting other horses from the stable. Last time he left Ligård he had seen the same fellows returning from a canter. They were absolutely first-class riders. He was going to be one, too, and quickly at that! And belong here, just like them.

A group of three riders let their horses step out through the gateway by the barn.

"The stables are on this side—the cowbarn is on the other side, but it's only used for storage," Sigrid explained. Mama, Ella, and she were waiting outside till the horses had passed through.

The riders nodded and smiled their thanks and went on their way chattering gaily with one another.

"See how they're looking forward to their ride!" Ella swiveled right around to have a good look at them and went backward in through the gateway.

The other two were through already; they had to stand and shade their eyes.

In the bright fall sunshine, colors, people, animals—all flickered and blended at first.

But not for Ella. "We're not the only ones who've come here to gape! The big girls over there, and those two people with the baby carriage, and—but there's Svein," she yelled.

"Hi, there, Svein!"

Sigrid jumped and went beet-red when Ella ran across and asked, "Is that your father?"

Mama looked rather surprised as she greeted a lean, elderly gentleman, who lifted his hat. The boy with the fair crew cut was all eyes for the horses—but he managed to move his neck a bit and make some sort of croaky noise.

He seemed to whisper something to his father, too, for he moved his stick over to his left hand and patted Ella on the head. "How's it going with the young lady —no bad aftereffects from being knocked down, I hope?"

"My daughter has not wanted to drive since," he said, turning toward Mrs. Tyrgrend. "She got quite a shock. How, eh—how fortunate that it turned out as it did," he added, as no one said anything. Then it dawned on him that this charming young mother had not heard anything about the accident.

She stood there, tense and pale, chewing her lower lip, but then she thrust her hands into her coat pockets and turned to face her daughters. "It was that evening she fell down in the mud, wasn't it?"

The brown eyes forced a nod from each of them. At that moment both mother's and elder daughter's cheeks started burning. How alike they were! The younger, on the other hand, firm little nut that she was, looked quite unruffled.

"Ha, we certainly don't hear very much from our children!" Father laughed nervously. How was he to smooth over this blunder of his?

"What a beautiful Sunday," he said conversationally. "And what a great life they have up here. We've just been talking to the owner of the stable, Svein and I. That's to say, the stable here belongs to the owner of the farm, but he lets it out for the horses, as far as I gather."

While Father went on talking to his not very interested audience, Svein said to the girls in a casual voice, "I'm going to start riding up here—once a week. If I can make enough myself, it'll be twice."

Only Sigrid heard the ring of excitement in his voice and saw how happy Svein's eyes were.

Ella had already run to Mama and tugged at her arm. "Won't you let us ride once a week, too?"

"I'm afraid we can't afford it, my dear." The words were spoken quietly, but not quietly enough.

"Oh, it's not too bad at all when you think what it must cost to keep up these horses!" Mr. Moen told them what he would be paying for Svein's riding lessons.

"That's all right. But I've got *two*. And we live in an

expensive furnished flat . . . " Mama Tyrgrend wasn't feeling particularly happy. It wasn't very pleasant to have to stand there and give an account of one's finances. And what's more, the little man over there with the mop of gray hair seemed to be listening. He had been stumping around them for some time on his short legs. But now he came right up to them. The nerve of him!

He made a half bow and rubbed his hands on his riding breeches, as if he intended to shake their hands.

"Excuse me, now. But this little one—wasn't it her that was thrown out so roughly by my stable lads the other day?"

Svein's father quickly introduced them, and Gunder explained he had driven into the farmyard just as Ella slipped out of it. The boys had reported the "chucking out," but they had a good lot of fun out of it!

"What!" Mama raised her eyes to heaven in mock despair. "If I'm going to hear any more about you, Ella, let's have it now."

Neither Ella nor Sigrid was impolite enough to remind her that she'd heard about *that*, at least. It wasn't so strange that Mama put on a bit of an air when two men were standing there paying attention to her.

The girls forgot to listen to the grownups' conversation, for whistling and teasing voices were heard through the gateway.

"Can I, Mama! Oh, please, can I!" It was Ella he was imitating, one of the boys. Sigrid thought she recognized him. Wasn't he the ginger-haired one who had talked to her that evening at the paper stand?

Svein got some words thrown at him, too. "What's up now, Svein? No time for your pals, uh? Not *you!* Gotta look after the girls!"

Had Svein grit in his mouth? He seemed to be chewing it anyway.

But Rolly and the other two boys didn't come inside the stable. Shortly afterward they were chased off by a tall bearded fellow whom they obeyed, strangely enough.

"We don't run a school exactly. But I show them a little, and they give a hand, those who come along here."

"Oh, certainly!" Mama shook Gunder's hand. She laughed, and her hair swung backward in regular Sigrid style. "Thank you very, very much. But really, it's almost too much."

Why was she so happy? Sigrid and Ella held their breath as everyone turned around toward them.

Gunder hawked and rubbed his twisted nose. "Well, girls. Come on up here, and we'll just see what's what." He winked craftily.

A whoop of joy made the black stallion rear up, so that the man with the beard had to leap around with the reins and get him under control.

Ella ran from Mama to Svein to Gunder, hugged everyone's arms, and crowed, "We'll just see, we'll just see, hee, hee!"

Sigrid just stood quietly, beaming her own joy—and perhaps a bit of Svein's, too.

His feet went crunch, crunch . . . on the crust of ice . . . over the puddles . . . along the farm road . . . up to Ligård.

It was the first ice Svein had seen this year . . . the first ice . . . the first time . . . he was going to ride.

His feet went crr-unch, crr-unch when he trod care-fully, for he was in no hurry, really.

His body tingled strangely all over. He didn't seem to have blood in his veins today. Soda, perhaps? No, fruit champagne!

When Svein went through the gateway, a new life would begin, he thought. It began right *now*, when he stepped into the farmyard.

No Rolly with his gang lounging along the walls? No, glad to say. Wouldn't have been much fun with a cheer gang like that—not the first time you got up on a horse.

He reached out his hand to open the stable door, but bang! Crash and clatter inside, and the door flew open.

"Whoa, whoa!"

A huge black horse's head was just in front of him— above him! Tramp, tramp! All Svein could do was to leap aside.

"There, now, boy, you'll soon get a chance to stretch yourself!"

Yes, it was Gunder coming backward and holding

the prancing stallion. Svein didn't see him at first—
thought the horse had broken loose.

But—surely Gunder didn't mean Svein was to ride
on *that* . . . on the biggest, wildest, craziest horse in
the whole stable!

Should he clear out, slink along the wall, and . . .
too late! Gunder had seen him and grinned.

"He isn't very patient, this one, not this guy. Easy
now . . . " Then he managed to tie the rope to the
ring in the wall. "Look out there!"

Svein shot to the side and avoided the hoofs that
flashed up. Only when the heavy hindquarters
thumped down again did he realize how near he had
come to getting a crack from the iron shoes.

"You must never go close behind a horse, son!"

Svein wasn't so sure any more that he ever wanted
to go near any horse again anywhere.

Oh, if, if, if only he didn't have to get up on that
one! It would be murder!

"Go in, will you, and make friends with Flora. And
ask Jens to come on out here and saddle Pronto."

"Jens?"

"The lanky weed with the awful beard. Tell him
he's to take Pronto and ride the worst off him."

Svein got no idea of what Jens looked like. He just
talked to something tall in a corner—something tall
that shambled past with harness over its shoulder.

He didn't see much of anything else either, just a
row of horses' rumps—big, broad horses' rumps on both
sides of the center aisle. Which of them was Flora's?

59

It must surely be a horse Gunder meant he was to get to know? A lady-horse that he was to ride?

There were many lady-horses—but none of them said, "My name is Flora." The little light-colored pony he quite fancied. It was smaller than the others and seemed pretty peaceful.

"Flora?" began Svein in wheedling tones. "Are you Flora?"

"No, this is Little Miss, this one. Didn't Jens tell you where Flora was?" Gunder led the way down along the line of rumps. "Here's the lady."

"Oh, thanks very much." She was pretty big—not so high as the monster outside there, but much bigger than Little Miss. Dark brown.

"A hackney," said Gunder. He came over with a pair of brushes.

"This here's the 'dandy,' and that's called the body-brush." So Svein was told to get rid of all the loose hair and dirt with the rough one—the one that looked like the stairbrush at home, only without the handle. After that he was to use the pot-scrubber one.

After having assured Svein that Flora was steady as a rock and never got up to any tricks, Gunder left him.

Now Svein was terrified of coming anywhere near the hind legs. He stole around them in as wide an arc as he could and took up his position fairly midway between them and the powerful rows of teeth. Were horses angry when they drew back their lips and blew through their teeth?

He made a little trial run with the brush down Flora's side. What a belly! Was it really possible to sit on such a barrel as this lady?

She turned her head and looked at him—just looked. But when he started his brushing again, Flora moved sideways in her stall. Toward him!

"Stop! Get back, or I'll be flattened!" Svein stood there squeezed tight against the partition. He pushed outward, but the colossus just pressed all the harder. Steady as a rock! It *was* a rock! No tricks—oh, no, just crushing a boy and trampling his toes to jelly.

Svein punched his clenched fists into Flora's flank, and at last the mountain of flesh moved slowly away.

Perhaps it was safer to try the other brush. She maybe liked it better. The body-brush had a band that fitted over his hand. Fine. Svein rubbed away at the dark coat.

Flora snorted and fussed. She took little steps, and her belly quivered.

"Can't you stand still for even one minute, you fat galoot!"

There was a giggle outside the stall.

"You must rub harder. Otherwise, you only tickle."

They looked as if they were enjoying themselves hugely, both Sigrid and Ella.

"When did you arrive?"

"Just now. Gunder's gone to get brushes for us, too."

"I'm to get Little Miss," crowed Ella. Well, at least someone was lucky.

"Well, so you should, as you're the smallest." Svein stretched out to the very last inch and stroked really hard with the "dandy." Oddly enough, Flora stood quite still then. OK, auntie, hard rubs you'll get.

Gunder nodded—yes, it was going fine there—when he went by with the gear for the other two. He came back later and showed Svein how to lift the horse's leg and get it to bend its knee.

"If you're to get her real clean in the little hole here under the hoof, you'll have to use one of these." With a kind of twig Gunder tweaked out muck and dried mud while he held the hoof tightly between his own knees.

It'd be some time before he'd lift one of these club legs, as heavy as lead, Svein promised himself. Suppose he got one on the nose.

For a while all was activity in the stable. The children worked away with the gear they had been given. The combing and brushing was done with great zest and determination.

If only the children knew, Gunder thought, how many tugs at the hair and clumsy grips in sensitive places were *not* paid back with bites or kicks. They were used to children, these horses, and almost unbelievably patient.

But the patience of the child grooming Little Miss was almost exhausted.

"Gunder, you promised we'd get a ride today! Didn't you, Gunder?"

"No, really, did I now?" Gunder was quite sure he could remember no such thing.

But, nonetheless, he did come, dragging quite a bit of harness. And it was just as well, for Ella's lips had begun to quiver.

"You won't manage the bridle and bit yourself, will you now, little one."

"*I* can do it!" Sigrid stuck her head out from Steady's stall. "I've done it at h . . . before. Often."

"OK, OK, have a go. But if he's good-tempered, Steady's certainly stubborn, too. His mouth isn't the easiest to get a bit into."

Sigrid was given all the harness, and then Gunder went in to Little Miss and Ella.

Svein patted Flora's neck with an almost steady hand. He should have had sugar or something with him to sweeten her up with—just as mother did when Svein had to do something he didn't like.

There was nothing in his pocket that he could offer her, not even a throat pastille. Ah, his lunch pack! He hadn't wanted his school food today. His bag was hanging on a peg in the back room, over there where they were putting up a huge stall, or whatever it was.

"Here, Flora!" Svein broke a piece in two and reached one of the halves out to the soft muzzle. "Do you like goat cheese?"

"Hey, son! Keep your hand flat!"

Gunder had seen the lunch pack being brought and sensed danger. Svein was told that they didn't keep any spare finger ends around the stable.

And he also heard a faint giggle from the girls again.

But there was no time to be annoyed, for Gunder

64

now stood ready with the bridle. Into the jaws with the bit, and up along the side of the cheeks with the straps—right behind the ears—and make fast!

"Next time you can do it yourself."

"You'll have to lay in some spare finger ends, then." Gunder laughed, but pointed out where there were gaps in the horse's gums. "Here's where you take hold if you want to open her jaws. But Flora's a *lady*. She knows how to behave."

Gunder backed her out of the stall while he explained that Flora had been a trotter in her early days. His blood ran cold, sure enough. But it wasn't just any old horse Svein was going to ride.

All right, then. But just now Svein merely wished the lady had been somewhat smaller. He took a long look at the neat little pony when Ella came by leading it.

"You can have a ride on Little Miss if you like, after I've finished!"

Could such cheeky little girls read one's thoughts? He just shook his head in utter contempt.

"You're a clever lass to manage Steady, and that's a fact!"

Sigrid came along proudly pulling her horse already bitted. "I fooled him with a bit of sugar," she said with a laugh.

"So we're all ready, then." Gunder clapped Flora on the rump and gave the reins to Svein. "It's usual to ride bareback first go—and the next few times. But I'll find some sort of cover for you."

They were told to go backward out of the stable door and lead the horses after them. Flora clumped willingly after Svein. It felt odd to walk with a real live horse on the reins!

Yet everything was so absolutely different from what he had supposed. This great heavy beast didn't really belong to the same family as the pony in the circus or the super-horse on the wall.

But there was something nice and friendly about Flora. She had kind eyes—he could see that now.

Whoa—stop! This fat old barrel had very nearly whipped off his toes! In the middle of the narrow doorway she speeded up suddenly, and Svein had to jump out sideways.

Did the girls start laughing again? Any smart remarks from them who knew everything so much better?

No. They had enough to do to control their own horses. There were others beside Svein who might yet need spare toes.

They found out the reason for it all outside.

The man called Jens came thundering back with the crazy stallion.

"Get Pronto right in, will you?" said Gunder. "He just makes trouble for us. And then you can give us a hand after."

"Right. But he's a real lamb now. And so lively!" His yellow beard shone in the sunlight.

He more or less steered the sweating lamb sideways,

but both Pronto and Jens did manage to get in through the stable door somehow.

Now it was easier to get the other horses to stand still. Gunder slapped a kind of rug onto each of them, making the dust rise in showers.

Bother, there sat Sigrid already astride Steady. How on earth had she managed it?

"Look, Svein, just stand on that block, and then take hold of the mane beside that bump there . . . " Her hands rested on Steady's withers.

It was all very well for a long-legged girl like her. But for others it was really pretty hopeless.

Gunder lifted Ella up on Little Miss. Was Svein to stand here and wait to be lifted up like another baby?

"Put your foot here." Suddenly the big bearded guy stood beside him, with his hands clasped in front of him.

A bit hesitantly Svein poked the toe of his rubber boot into the offered hands.

"Hold tight. Hip, there!" Hip it was! That really was quite a flip!

Anyway, there sat Svein on horseback for the first time in his life.

"Hold 'em this way." The reins were twisted through his fingers. "Pull in a bit if she begins to walk off."

"Are you going?"

"I'll just water Pronto. Be right back. There's nothing to worry about, kid."

No. There probably wasn't. But it was mighty far

down to the ground. And it did happen that folk fell off.

Yes, indeed! That's just what he was doing right now! Flora bent her neck. Help! She went straight down in front—he was going to slide off!

Get your head up, old hag! He heaved and tugged at the reins; it must surely be possible to lift a head like that. Aha, here we are. Now it's back in its place, but . . .

The whole huge body began to sway. It moved under Svein; it walked away!

He clung as tightly as he could with his legs and pulled harder, but Flora didn't stop. She was wrongly adjusted. She went backward!

A "Whoa!" from Gunder stopped the ghastly sea-roll.

"Why are you going back?"

"I'm just trying to hold her in . . ."

"You're directing her back when you pull like that." Gunder was leading Little Miss, but if Jens hadn't come steaming up with a seven-league stride, both the misses would have had to look after themselves.

"Are you trying to rip the old girl's mouth to bits? She'll soon split right up to the ears the way you're going on!"

Jens read the lesson about how tender horses were at the edge of the mouth—it didn't take long to injure them.

"Hands light as a feather—that's the first rule hereabouts." Then he took the reins.

Who was he to be so uppish? Gunder was the boss,

wasn't he! Svein didn't at all like being led by this woolly head who called him "kid." In fact, he didn't like being led at all! Sigrid out in front there, she was allowed to jog along on her own, without anyone's holding Steady on a leading rein!

But there were one or two things he had to learn. "Does it all mean something to the horses, everything you do with arms or legs?"

"With all of you. I'm telling you. You don't just sit there and pull the strings as if the horse was Punch 'n Judy. He senses all you do. In fact, you can bet he knows what you're thinking, too!"

Jens's sleepy eyes beneath the curly thatch right beside Svein's shoulder—perhaps they really weren't so sleepy after all, just a bit heavy in the lids. Svein got answers to all his questions, clear and straightforward ones. Maybe the instructors in the Riding Club expressed themselves differently. But Svein felt that this bearded guy *liked* horses, and that was more important than how he talked.

While Jens explained, Flora swayed around the yard, around and around. Svein was no longer so dizzy and seasick, and he managed to nod quite convincingly when Ella shouted, "Isn't it *fun*, Svein!"

The sky had clouded over, but Ella was a good-enough sun.

"So it isn't just to jump on a horse, dig your heels in, and be off!" Jens concluded.

Svein understood that much now. This was something that had to be learned, just like cycling, skiing, skating—everything that had something to do with balance.

"Can I try to go myself now?"

"Would you dare, kid? I'd better walk beside you and catch you when you slide off." Svein was pretty sure he saw a grin in the beard, but he got the reins back.

"Relax your back and rump. Let yourself go with her rocking. Feel which leg moves when. And, remember you're going *forward*. And no pulling back, now, or . . . "

Jens's clenched fist still hung in the air as a danger signal as Svein carefully pressed his knees together and clicked "go" with his tongue.

Flora obeyed! She rolled along after Steady and Little Miss, and the rider was quite sure it was his will that drove her forward—until they stopped for a moment in front there, and Flora stopped, too, without Svein's having given any order or had anything to do with it at all.

He began to suspect that there were possibly two wills playing this game. But when the procession was off again—and Flora joined it before Svein had even *thought* of giving a start signal—then he realized that there was only one will. And it was not his. Fortunately, no one else could know.

As a matter of fact, it was rather nice to be carried forward like this. Lovely, it was!

He had his balance completely under control, really. Only occasionally he had to catch hold of the mane.

"Hello there, Sigrid!" He managed an impressive wave on the turn. It did no harm to let her see that others could ride, too.

She didn't seem to notice that he heeled over slightly just then on the rounded back.

"You're doing fine!" A smile and a wave back.

But Jens wasn't *quite* so considerate. "Are you trying to pull her hairs up by the root?"

So soft . . . so smooth and nice! Could there be anything in the world nicer to feel against your hand than a horse's muzzle, than this particular muzzle that snuffed and snaffled right up his arm to find more sugar?

"Sigrid had only three pieces to spare," Svein muttered in Flora's ear. "Next time I'll bring some myself. Lots!"

The big dark head nuzzled affectionately against his shoulder, while the ears seemed to be pricked in order to hear all he whispered.

"You are the best horse in the world! I'll never call you 'fat galoot' or 'barrel belly' again!"

It had been easy to take off the bridle—Jens had stood watching mainly. It was nothing at all to put on the halter. She had been watered, and she had been brushed down. Now there was nothing for it but to say good-bye. A last hug against the warm neck, and then Svein had to leave the stable.

In the back room there was hammering and sawing. Gunder and Jens had nearly finished Pronto's box.

"Bye for now."

"Be seeing you, kid."

The girls had asked if they would all go together on the streetcar. But Svein wanted to go home by himself.

Svein bounced out of Ligård with quite a different step than when he had arrived. Hands behind his back, head erect—head that seethed with thoughts about horses.

Then someone said, "Heigh, ho!"

Where from? From the top of the wall. There sat Rolly astride, grinning.

"You were sure good at being towed around the farmyard. Quite some show! Are you gonna join the circus?" He jumped down and began to saunter along beside Svein down the road.

"I thought you and your two sweeties would be going to ride here. It's OK for those with a pa stinking with dough. And how Gunder melts when a dear little mum sets her great big eyes on him! You bet, he just melts like coconut fat. It's sure different for the kids who've been around here for years begging to get in an odd job to pay for a lesson or two. Oh, no thanks! Then it's *full* up! Then it's just call again, sonny boy, when the others are pensioned off. What a louse!" Rolly spat out. "What a lousy snob."

"Gunder? Surely he is not a snob even if . . . "

"Gunder's both a snob and a great deal more I happen to know about." Rolly took care that Svein should

72

know about it, too. He stuck like a burr all the way down. He slandered Gunder and Jens and everybody connected with the stable, in the foulest way—even the horses. They were rotten, fit only for the sausage machine.

Why should Rolly always pick on *him*, Svein wondered. He had plenty of cronies to hang around with, for Rolly knew just about everybody. All the tough guys, at least.

"Have a fag, uh?"

Svein merely shook his head. And so he heard the same old story. He didn't care to tell Rolly that his eyes smarted and began to water like a sniffly child's when he smoked. So it wasn't because he was too noble that he refused.

The suggestion about the movies came next. He turned that down, too.

"Go home to Mumsie then. She'll sure hold her nose. You stink of mare for miles."

Rolly was right there, though.

"Go and put something else on, and *wash* yourself!"

But he wasn't going to wash off the smell of Flora. And, fortunately, the clothes kept the smell in his room that day and the day after.

The horse bug—it really had bit him hard.

Sigrid was frying pancakes. Ella sat hunched up on the tall stool and enjoyed the sight.

"Get back a bit—it's spluttering!"

"It's spitting, just like Ragnhild's cat when she had kittens."

"By the way, you didn't need to tell all that to Gunder—about where we came from."

"Well, he aksed me!" Her brown eyes looked hurt from beneath the forelock.

" 'Asked' we say. You don't trouble about anything any more. Not about speaking or . . . "

"But when he as-ked if we came from a fe-farm, as we were so good with horses, I couldn't have said we didn't, could I? I really had to say our house was just beside Rud, didn't I? And that we were as much on the farm as the Rud boys themselves?"

Sigrid turned the pancake carefully. It went over, but only just.

"We *agreed* that we wouldn't say anything. As soon as you begin telling about our house and all that, everybody begins to snoop and ask things."

"That doesn't matter, surely!"

Then Mama came into the kitchen—she had just been changing into her house clothes.

"Lovely, Sigrid! Is that the last? You're smarter than I am with pancakes. Have you laid the table, Ella?"

An unnecessary question, as only the red-checked tablecloth lay on the table.

Ella jumped down from the stool with a bump. There was a rattling and tinkling as glasses, cutlery, and plates were set pretty quickly on the table.

"Mind you don't break anything. We've got to replace everything, you know. It's not much fun using other people's things."

Ella knew about a little blue bowl that wasn't in its place in the cupboard any more and thought it might be better to find something pleasanter to talk about.

"We were riding on a rope today! Gunder held the end of mine, and Little Miss ran around and around, and I turned on her back! She liked it. I could feel she was happy!"

They sat down to table, and Sigrid told that she had learned to use her legs and heels.

"Oh!" Mama couldn't help smiling. "Is it fun, then, pets?"

"It's *real*. Animals *are* real."

"Not folk, you think?"

"Not city folk anyway," said Ella firmly.

"It was lovely that Grandpa said he would pay one lesson a week for you. But you seem to be up there two or three times a week anyway—you're not running up there too often, are you?"

"Oh, no. Gunder says we're just to come. It's a help to him!"

"Yes, indeed! He says we work like real stable hands. And we don't run about fooling with the boys, like the other girls. May I have the jam, please?" Ella was ready for her second helping.

"There you are."

"It's only now and again Gunder has time to teach us anything, like today."

"Well, well. Have you gotten to know many others up there, then? Others besides Svein?"

"Oh, *yes*, we have!" Mama got a description of Jens and Martin and Per-Erik. They had also met some girls —big girls.

"Aren't *they* 'real,' then?"

"Sure. People who look after animals are almost."

Mama laughed. "You've got your own system for dividing people, you really have, Ella."

"Her own system for eating jam, too," Sigrid said sharply. "Do you mind leaving just a *little*, please."

Pancake number two was placed like a carpet on top of the dollop of blueberry jam. "But there's *one* boy who's not at all real. He's not in the stable, though, for he isn't allowed in, I think."

"Where is he then?"

"He hangs around outside. When we go home, he often follows us."

"What?" Mama sat there with her fork halfway to her mouth, her neck bent. She looked like a pointer showing a bird.

"Take it easy—he isn't dangerous." Sigrid steered the fork down.

"Oh, no, he's just showing off and making up to Sigrid."

"Oof, don't be silly."

"Asks her to the movies, and . . . "

"Eat up, first." But Ella hadn't had so much pancake in her mouth that her news had not been understood. And Mama certainly didn't look very soothed.

"You surely haven't been to the movies with him?" Mama asked worriedly.

"Are you *mad*? Rolly is so nasty—really awful."

The roses on her cheeks that always gave Sigrid away made it clear that Rolly was a bit thrilling, in spite of everything.

"It's best to keep away from boys like that. They are so much more forward here in the city than . . . " Mama hesitated and then continued. " . . . than the boys at Rud and the others from Bakken."

She peered anxiously from the younger girl to the older one.

Ella burst out laughing! "Ha, ha, ha! Think of Erland at the Christmas party!"

Sigrid had looked gloomy for a moment, but then her cheeks began to twitch, too.

"Oh, yes, poor Erland . . . " With her napkin in front of her mouth, Mama assured them it *was* naughty to laugh, but . . .

The recollection of the little freckled boy who was so terribly embarrassed that he ran away to the storeroom because he was scared to hold the girls' hands in the Farmer in the Dell—this made all three of them collapse with laughing.

"And his auntie came dragging him along," Ella said with a whoop.

"And joined him up with big fat Eline!" gasped Mama.

"Who hung on to him for the rest of the party," added Sigrid, giggling.

It was the first time they had laughed together about something that happened before they moved to town. This laughter was a good step forward, thought Mama, in the direction they would have to go.

"But the day you're more interested in the boys at Ligård than in the horses, then that's the end of your trips up *there!*"

The fork was now waving again.

But they laughed a little at that, too.

What a horrible bump-bump-bumpity-bump.

"You'll be hacked away to chops and steaks. Your teeth are just for spitting out, and your innards will follow."

These were the words of comfort Svein got on the way, along with a broad, bearded grin.

They were on their first ride outside Ligård. The road sloped gently through fir woods, past little houses with leafy gardens. It was misty, and a fine rain was falling, but that was nothing. He had his raincoat.

Gunder had asked them to sit down as much as possible when they were trotting, but this was just about the time when that wasn't possible any more.

This drive was fine for turning into. Svein held Flora back a little and eased her gently out to the right. Now that they knew each other and were friends, they agreed, Flora and he. Most of the time, anyway.

Then came what he was waiting for. Pronto came snorting and prancing past.

"Are you wanting a bit of recuperation?" Gunder asked. The gray eyes shot a quick glance to see if everything was all right.

"Oh no." Svein didn't even know what it meant. "But I think Flora would rather not have Pronto behind her."

"And here I'm trying to make a gentleman of him . . . teach him to go well mannered behind the mares!"

It was pretty tough work even for Gunder to check Pronto in one spot for any length of time. His neck was tensed like a bow at full stretch, and his hoofs were digging deeply into the road.

"Oh, well, then, walk on and take the lead." The bow straightened, and Pronto shot forward. "*Walk*, I said! We'll have no gallops here, you villain!"

Svein heard no more. But he saw that Little Miss and Steady speeded up out there in front, even though Pronto just passed them at a quick trot.

Great! Now Flora and Svein could do what they wanted, without having watching eyes behind them.

It *was* much easier. Find the rhythm, and rise up after every second step. Up-down, up-down. No more of the hard bumpity-bump.

They were only going to ride around a little circuit today—just up to the new housing development and down the other side. Work was over for the weekend, and the traffic had eased off.

Little Miss was a good bit in front. The white tail

had just vanished around a heap of crushed stones from one of the new buildings.

Svein had let Flora slow down to a walk, but now he drove her forward again, pressed his heels in, thrust his own body forward, and slackened the reins a fraction.

"Good girl, trot a bit now. We've got to catch up with the others."

Flora did more than that.

Something white came rolling down the steep slope —clatter, clatter, clatter against the stones.

Flora—oh, no, what are you doing—don't rear! Svein clutched her neck with both arms and stood upright in the stirrups. Then down he plumped—still in the saddle. The white thing rolled out into the road.

Flora's whinny shattered his ears. She leaped to the

side—away from the white thing. And off she went!

Tatta tatt, tatta tatt, tatta tatt—this was galloping!

Another noise—besides the hoofbeats—but Svein had more than enough to do to hang on. He was stretched out in air—so it seemed—with his head against Flora's neck.

Heaps of stones, trees, and telegraph poles streamed by . . . a terrified face. Ella's mouth wide open. "Ohhhh . . . "

"Svein!" Sigrid's eyes, dark, frightened . . .

"Hey! Whoa!" Pronto's head up beside them . . . the reins . . . whoosh!

Svein soared in a wide curve. Hospital—broken neck —Mother, Father by his bedside—ow!

There he lay in the ditch. But he didn't seem to have

broken anything. There were both withered grass and fallen leaves to soften his fall.

He was sitting picking nasty wet leaves from himself when Gunder came back on Pronto, with Flora on the reins.

Flora! That shivering horse that struggled and pulled to get loose?

Ears back, eyes staring wildly, mouth tense, half open, and nostrils distended. Was *that* Flora?

"Everything all right, son?"

Svein nodded and stood up.

"I thought I'd have managed to slacken her down slowly. But she leaped like a goat the minute I got hold of the reins."

"Yes." Svein had noticed it himself.

"What frightened her like that?" Gunder's gray mane stood on end, too, with its streak of white like a comb.

Yes, what was it? How did it all begin? The streak of hair gave Svein the clue.

"It was something white! Something white came clattering down the slope. Looked like a bowl, or pitcher, but it didn't break."

"A white pitcher?" The words were rapped out.

"Uh? Yes, I think so. Flora? Hey, Flora! *Nothing* to worry about!" Svein was allowed to take the reins. He trotted along beside his frightened horse. He patted and stroked her wherever he could, checked her little by little until at last she stood still.

He rested his head against her shoulder and put his

arms protectively around her neck. He felt how her alarm faded away and heard her heart beat more quietly. Whether it was his own or Flora's, he couldn't tell.

Sigrid and Ella paced their horses slowly backward and forward a little distance away. They were looking across at Svein the whole time and were dying with curiosity, but they didn't dare come near Flora yet. They had both had a bit of a gallop as well, but had managed to rein in their horses. Gunder praised them for that.

He had tied Pronto to a pole and walked back to see what had fallen onto the road. Now he came back, his face grim.

"Sure, it *was* a white pitcher." He opened his raincoat a little and showed Svein, behind Flora's back, a dented, chipped enamel water pitcher.

Svein didn't get it. What was so awful about that pitcher? Why did Gunder take it with him? Why had peaceful Flora gone so completely off her head? It was reasonable enough that she should take fright when something fell toward her with a clatter and a clash—but so absolutely out of her wits?

No, there was something strange here.

"You can sit up on her now, if you want. If you dare, I mean!" Not the usual sly Gunder smile—just a gloomy look. But he helped Svein up into the saddle.

It was not until he sat there that Svein noticed how tender his rear was.

"Come along after Pronto, now. But not *too* near, or he'll kick."

They got back to the stable all right.

When the horses were in their stalls and Pronto in his new box in the back, Gunder came in. He had the pitcher under his arm.

"Get rid of it so *nobody* can find it again!" he said gruffly to Jens.

And Jens took it, nodded just as seriously, and went out of the stable. The girls had barely had time to tell him what had happened.

That Saturday they went home together, for Sigrid and Ella also wanted to walk.

They saw nothing of Rolly, which certainly didn't make anyone sorry.

"Are you sure you haven't hurt yourself, Svein?" Sigrid was still wide-eyed and pale. She reminded Svein of the fairy tale "Snow White and Rose Red." Only she was both of them, by turns.

He assured them he was just fine. "Only a bit sore. Quite a bit."

"Yes, awful. I'll eat lunch *standing*. But wasn't it exciting, all those things happening today?" Ella shuddered deliciously. "Weren't you frightened?"

"Sure was. But I don't *understand*." Svein walked on lost in thought, his hands in his pockets.

He didn't see the girls exchanging looks and nodding to each other.

"Are *you* looking forward to next weekend, Sigrid?" Ella picked red leaves from a grapevine at the edge of the road. It was hanging down from a fence.

"I don't know. It'll be so . . . different." Both glanced at Svein, but he didn't look up—didn't ask any questions.

"We're going back home to Bakken, where we used to live, on a visit! Next Friday! And we're staying till Monday."

"We're visiting our father." Now it was Sigrid who dared to speak up.

"Oh, yes." Svein began to think of the noise he had heard, besides Flora's galloping.

"Mama and Papa are going to be divorced. That's why we have moved here."

"I see." Somebody had been laughing. That's what it sounded like! Up there on the slope. A cold, mocking laughter.

Could it be . . . ? Had someone thrown the pitcher down at the horses? At Flora? Oh, no. No one did things like that, surely. Deliberately?

Was there some connection between Flora and the pitcher?

Why should anyone have wanted to scare Flora in particular? Or—was it *him*, Svein, they were out to get? *Who* was out to get him?

A shiver went down his spine. There was something fishy here, at any rate.

He said good-bye to the girls outside his door and had not the faintest idea that an important experiment had been carried out on the way down. And it was entirely due to him that the experiment had succeeded.

"Oh, dear, let's air the place!" Mother gasped. "Even when you've changed your clothes, Svein, it *reeks* of horse in here."

"Just so. I feel I'm really in a stable here," Father said. "May I have some more oats? I mean cake. Ha, ha!"

No joyous response from Svein. Mother passed the cake dish.

"You *won't* get any lumps of sugar, though, for, would you believe it, the bag is empty again!" Mother glanced mischievously at Svein over the rim of her coffee cup.

"I'll go up to my own room, and then you'll get rid of the smell." What *they* said had certainly gotten through.

"Don't be upset, Svein dear! We're just joking, you know. Do sit down here and have a nice time. After all, it's Saturday evening!"

"Tell us how you made out at riding today." It must surely be possible to get a word or two out of the boy, his father thought.

"I was thrown off." Some words!

"What are you *saying!*" Up sprang Mother to see if he was all right. He got a little hug into the bargain.

"Well, a really experienced rider has to be thrown

off ten times, hasn't he? Or is it seven?" Father lit his Saturday cigar.

"Don't know. But I've a good chance of being an experienced rider pretty soon."

His parents received no answer when they asked what he meant by that.

Svein clenched his teeth and rose from the sofa. He forced himself to walk with ordinary, easy strides toward the door.

"Heavens! Does it hurt *so* much!" cried Mother, and clasped her hands together. "You'd better sleep with compresses on tonight!"

She should have seen him outside the door, after it was closed. Or walking up the stair! That really hurt!

Two aching sticks were what he had for thighs, and they felt flayed, too, in a few "exposed places." He probably looked even more wretched than Mother during one of her worst rheumatic attacks.

Halfway up he stood stock-still. Had Mother really *so* much pain when she walked upstairs? She certainly didn't complain very much. But surely no one would walk as he was now, dragging his legs behind him, unless it was absolutely necessary. He was going to run up the stairs for her now each time she was taken poorly. So far he hadn't done much of that.

The super-horse on the wall received all the questions he had been churning over in his mind all afternoon. It looked back at him, staring him in the eye with sharp warning:

"Be careful! Keep a good lookout! Anything can happen!"

Down in the living room Mother sighed. "We should have TV, don't you think? Then he would be more downstairs with us."

Father pulled some wry faces. "You have no sooner terrorized me into paying for riding lessons than you pitch in again with the old TV story. The time's not *that* far off when I reach my pension, and we'll have to have *something* at our backs . . . "

"Retirement age."

"Beg pardon?"

"You reach your *retirement age*."

"That's just what I'm *saying*. Ohh!" A fleck of tobacco from his tongue was blown sharply in the direction of the ashtray. "And what have we gotten for all we've put out on his riding? There is not much visible evidence of his gratitude. Nor is he noticeably livelier!"

"Oh, he's up and down. But it's probably going to take a bit longer to show. Before there are any— results."

Mrs. Moen couldn't remember if there had been anything in the book about how long it would take before the treatment took effect and the children became happy. But she hadn't entirely lost her strong faith in the book she had showed Lena.

There must surely be *some* truth in books like that. Otherwise, why did people write them?

Svein had a feeling of being watched, as in detective mysteries, when he reached the farm, but inside the stable he felt safer.

Lazy munching at the last wisps of hay, now and then a stamp, and the friendly warmth from the horses —none of that was at all upsetting. It was quite incredible how much more peaceful it had become inside here now that Pronto had been moved out to his "single room," as Gunder and Jens called his box in the back room.

Two other boys and Svein had worked for a good long spell, shovelling out reeking, damp sawdust and carrying in fresh pailfuls to the stalls. Torkel and Per-Erik had now gone, and Svein was busy getting Flora ready for a little outing.

The bridle was in its proper place, and the bit lay over the tongue in the toothless gap. *How* Svein had struggled the first time to get the bit *under* Flora's tongue, for Jens had said that that was very important.

Poor Flora had backed and flung her head and stuck out her neck. Svein saw too late that Jens was standing grinning in his beard. If it had been a false one, he would have yanked it off. What a gargoyle!

But you got used to Jens's wisecracks. He *was* a great guy.

Now, for instance, when Svein was struggling with the heavy saddle, Jens came whistling along and helped him to sling it properly across. But first he checked to see that it was clean underneath.

"If there's any dirt underneath there, she'll get chafed."

"I know." Svein tightened the saddle girth himself and drew it tight once or twice.

"I'll take it in one when you're up, outside. Flora's not fond of corsets."

"How right you are," thought Svein, as he remembered the times that both boy and saddle had slipped down the side when he had tried to swing himself up by the stirrup—for Flora had first filled herself with air, and when she let it out again, the girth became so slack that the whole thing just slid around. Almost all the horses tried that trick, but Flora was extra plump, and it was difficult to judge her size.

"You'll soon be moving on to something with more life than this old gal." The old gal got an affectionate tug on her mane and gave Jens in return a good-natured dunt with her head. They weren't exactly sworn enemies, these two.

"She was lively enough for me last time—more than enough."

"Ha!" Now both sets of teeth were visible. "She sure got a move on that day. And you fell on your puss."

"What was all that about the white pitcher, Jens? Why was Flora so scared of it?"

"Huh, well." His elbow came to rest on the partition, and the bearded chin settled into his hand. His long form flopped joint by joint, as if someone had relaxed the strings he was supported by.

"Well, you see, once we had a clearing out in the loft in the barn. Last year it was, before the hay was going in there. We heaved out a good lot of rubbish, and this pitcher flew out through an opening and came down on the midden. Bang! There it hit a stone and shot like a ball right against the legs of Flora, who was just coming up the track at the back there with an old hen on her back! Flora gave a start, of course, and was away, and if she'd flung the old girl like she flung you last time, there might not have been so much fuss. But those that deserve a trip into the ditch stay put. The old girl yelled and hollered and clawed and kicked and I don't know what. So when we got hold of Flora, she was quite beside herself."

"Poor Flora." She got some sympathetic pats on her neck.

"In all the fuss we forgot to get rid of the pitcher, and some kids pinched it. And, believe it or not, some of them were out once or twice after and waved the pitcher when Flora was standing outside alone. They thought it was great fun to see her go mad, you know. When Gunder heard about it, he cursed and swore and told them off in a way they won't forget very soon. And the pitcher was dug down. And it's only Gunder and me and one other person that knows where it was put."

"Where the pitcher was buried?"

"Yep." Jens straightened himself again and stepped aside so that Svein could get Flora backed out of the stall.

"Who was the one who knew it, apart from yourselves?"

"You'll have to stay in the farmyard today. It's too risky to let Flora and you out for a walk alone."

Jens wouldn't reply to the question he had been asked. He held the door open for horse and boy and pretended he hadn't heard.

After having made sure there was nothing suspicious about the farmyard, Svein led Flora out.

"What have you done with your girls this time?" A crumpled packet of cigarettes was removed from Jens's hip pocket.

"They *aren't* mine. Gone visiting their father. Don't help me. Just hold her, please."

When the stirrups were right down, Svein just managed to slip his toe in. He took a good hold of the saddle, and heave!—heave!—ho!

The third time he managed to get in such a good thrust that he could scramble astride Flora's back. Ow! His soreness hadn't all gone.

"You've got what it takes, kid." Jens blew the smoke almost horizontally from the corner of his mouth as he adjusted the stirrups and tightened the girth. "You'll have to bear another hole, Flora."

"May I ride in the avenue?"

"If you do, you'll have to take the shovel and clean up the muck afterward. What if any of the fancy secretaries from the office dirtied their best shoes!" The last came out in dainty tones.

You never knew with Jens what was wisecracking and what wasn't. But right now he was taking an unusually keen look in all directions before he opened the white gate and let Flora out into the farmyard.

"Keep your eyes open, kid!"

That made two of them who sniffed trouble in the breeze.

"Could there be something else Flora's afraid of?"

"Plenty. Anything could fright a horse if you really wanted. I'll let the gate stand open." Then Jens strode across the yard.

Was he perhaps going to see if the pitcher was well enough hidden?

Who *was* the third? Why hadn't he told Svein? It wasn't just because the temperature was below freezing and he had nothing on his hands that Svein shivered.

He glanced at each ornamental shrub, scrutinized each rosebud—in case there should be anything lurking in their winter covering of branches.

He let Flora walk at a leisurely pace down the avenue.

A haze lay over the city, and only the tops of the highest apartment houses and church steeples stuck out above the light layer of cloud. The view up here really was super.

At the entrance to the drive by the big gateposts Flora and Svein halted. He stretched himself and had a look upward to the right. No. He saw a row of identical little houses and a few nursery school children being dragged home by their mothers.

To the left, then? There the road twisted its way down toward the station and newspaper stand. He could not see as far as that, for bushes grew densely along the edge of the road on the other side. A truck was passing at that moment, but there was nothing suspicious about that.

So Svein turned Flora around, and just as he did, he heard it—the laughter. The same laughter as last time up on the slope, cold, mocking.

Flora had also heard it! There was no need to do anything to make her trot. He went bumpity-bump-bump upward again, but Svein didn't notice if it hurt or not this time.

He recognized the laughter! He was quite sure he did.

But . . . no. It didn't make sense. Rolly couldn't possibly have been one of the three who had buried the pitcher. What reason could *he* have had for being involved?

Some of the office people looked out of the windows in the main building when they heard the hoofbeats again. Could the laughter have come from one of them? Out of the window?

Hoofbeats . . . was it an echo? Or was he becoming completely jumpy and nervous? Svein listened. Yes, there *were* other clack-clacks beside Flora's. Was his enemy coming to meet him on horseback?

Around the corner of the building he saw Jens, Jens on Brage . . . dark brown, shaggy, big, lumbering Brage.

"Come here." Jens waved, and neither Svein nor Flora had any objection to obeying.

But Svein was quite stunned when Jens asked if they might exchange horses and take a little turn together.

Swap Flora?

Then it dawned on him that maybe Jens wanted to ride Flora to see if anyone would scare her then. If the same "somebody" was out to get that particular horse, then it was safest that the reins should be taken by the one with the best hold.

"You'll have to hold him a bit firmly. He's been at the timber in the woods for many years, so he gets speed up something terrific."

Had Svein ever thought that Flora was big!

Compared with this piece of mammoth machinery here, she was just a speck. And the steps Brage took! He had a long swinging and dragging motion. It was quite different from sitting on Flora.

Svein found his arms slightly cramped from holding the powerful beast in check, but he managed it. There was no use trying to get his head up; his neck had probably gotten this forward stretch from all the timber pulling.

Once they got out of the stable yard, Svein had to hold onto the saddle and lean backward going down the steep earth slopes. It was quite tricky—he had never ridden downhill at such a speed before.

Jens obviously hadn't noticed anything. Was he thinking of going across the footbridge and up the hill to the road behind the market garden?

Yes, he was. There was Flora, crossing very nicely. How could you get this forest troll to keep his balance on the narrow planks? His hoofs were about as big as hot plates.

Brage, in fact, had been doing some quiet thinking about the footbridge for himself. He checked so sharply that Svein almost slid off, and he would not budge.

"Don't take any nonsense!" bawled Jens from higher up the slope on the other side.

It was all very well for *him* to say so.

Heels in Brage's sides, then some hup-hups, and a bit of tongue clicking. Nothing doing. Brage turned himself across the path.

You *will*. Svein squeezed at the back with his left leg and in front with his right. He screwed the horse around with all the strength he had in his own body. It was like steering an enormous heavy iron sledge. But, Brage gave way to the pressure! He moved his hindquarters little by little until he stood with his nose facing the bridge.

And so: slap on the rump, dig, dig in with his heels, and hup, hup, hup, until his mouth was dry. With a great thundering clatter Brage was across!

"Fine, kid! You're not exactly the most hopeless case we've had up here. If you're not careful, you'll *learn* this game some day!"

Flora's curly top hair nodded assent.

Svein had never heard lovelier words. No doubt about it, Brage was a great horse, too! Just look at the way he took the steep bank at the road here. Well, he slid back down again because the grit was so loose. But they got up! He dug in deep and climbed!

While the horses were trotting easily along the motor road from the market garden, there was a roar behind them. They didn't normally worry, for they were used to traffic. But the muffler had been removed from this motor scooter, and both Flora and Brage put back their ears.

You never heard such a din! Now it was right behind. . . . Hold the reins tightly . . .

Hrummh! Help! The scooter shaved Brage—it wasn't an inch from his hind leg!

Svein had to do everything to hold his seat and follow Brage's terrified leaps to the side, but in front he heard, "You filthy punk!" and a string of other abusive words. Jens fired a shattering volley after the boys on the scooter.

The horses weren't quiet until they were back home again in the farmyard.

"Did you see who the boys on the scooter were?" Svein's stomach and bowels had turned to ice, for it was him, Svein, they were after—none of the horses.

"Uh-huh. I know the one at the back—Rolly's his name."

He was sure, for he had caught a glimpse of ginger hair and the evil grin.

"Ha! Guess who's going to taste this one!" Jens's clenched fist was brandished as he jumped down from Flora.

While they were stabling the horses, he told Svein about Rolly.

He was the youngest of an earlier riding class. He had been around the stable here for years, ever since Gunder came to Ligård. The rest of the boys had fallen away as they found other things to do, but not Rolly. He was as keen about horses as ever—and handy, too. "But crazy wild like a tornado! He was mad that Gunder talked hard to him several times. He grew uppish, you see."

One day in the spring he'd been furious—nobody knew why. And then he had ridden one of the mares so hard that she lost the foal she was carrying. "The vet could do nothing. It was *out*, all right, for Rolly then. But I can't see why he should hate *you* so much!"

Svein thought he knew—some of the reasons, at least.

Rolly probably felt that Svein had taken his place. And he had been annoyed before that because Svein had never wanted to join up with him. Who would ever have guessed that Rolly had been one of the riders before he began to hang around the street corners.

And something else, too: Rolly was keen on Sigrid—anyone could see that. And she—both girls, in fact—preferred to go home with Svein. They *asked* to go along with him to avoid Rolly!

So there were plenty of reasons.

It could be dangerous.

What a freezing wind was blowing on this platform! Her light coat was far too thin, but so far she had gotten only the girls' winter clothes organized.

What would they be like when they returned? Weepy? Ready to go back to the country with the first train? Grumpy, or solemn and quiet? Under control, so she wouldn't notice how much they were longing for the farm?

She shivered as she waited there, on edge while her hair blew over her eyes and her toes froze. Her cigarettes had been left at home.

The signal on the track changed to green. A voice droned something through the loudspeaker.

The stubby electric locomotive grew quickly in size, and here came the whole train, speeding, slowing down, stopping. The doors banged open, and out into the grayish white winter day tumbled the whole human content of the train. Suitcases, rucksacks, toddlers, and string bags were bundled down. People hurried past, with luggage of all shapes and sizes.

There was Sigrid, coming carefully down the tall steps with her bag. Then an about-turn to catch Ella, who more or less jumped into the air.

"Mama! Here we are!" was announced to the whole platform. And their hugs of welcome were certainly heartfelt.

"Fancy there being *snow* here! There was none there!"

"It didn't begin to be white until we were nearly in!"

Both girls slid happily on the thin covering of snow in the street.

"Greetings from Papa," Sigrid said, remembering.

"Thanks. Was everything all right?"

"Oh, yes. Grandma and Aunt Gunhild have moved into the house. Did you know?"

"Yes, I did."

"Don't say anything more about that. *Don't!*" she said to herself. Then she said aloud, "Had you a nice time, then, girls?"

"Oh, sure, we did. It was all so strange, though."

"I didn't try to think about it, for if we'd had *too* nice a time, then . . . "

"Then you wouldn't have found it easy to come back?"

Nod—a face lighting up. "But then I longed so *horribly* . . . "

Mama's heart missed a beat.

" . . . for Little Miss."

"Me, too. For Steady." To judge from the blushing face, the attraction was not *only* Steady.

But right now Mama quietly blessed both horses and boys at Ligård.

"Are you still going to marry Paul, Sigrid?"

"No, not Paul! A long-haired useless gowk like him?"

Ella giggled.

Her big sister put down the currycomb and began to tidy Steady's mane before she said anything else.

Little Miss had a moment's respite from the well-meaning treatment with the body-brush. When the pause for thought was over, there came from her stall: "At Bakken they think it's more strange, too, about dividing."

"Divorce, you mean?"

"Uh, huh. There must be more of that here. Another one in my class, anyway. But with her parents it was a long time ago."

"Have you talked to her about it?"

"Sure. You saw what happened with Svein. He didn't care about it at all. Didn't pity us or anything."

"It's different with Svein. He's so tactful and wouldn't want to pester us with questions, you see."

"Are you going to marry *Svein*, maybe, Shreddy? Tee-hee!"

"If you call me that name once more, you'll get the water bucket on your bean!"

How embarrassing! Svein had just come in a moment before. He hadn't gotten around to shouting hello to the girls at once or to going over to them in the stalls. Now he couldn't possibly show himself.

He pressed close against the wall. He bent double and sneaked along below the level of the stalls, all the way down. If the stable had been a few yards longer, he'd have been *stuck* like that—bent double.

The door to the rear of the stable fortunately opened soundlessly. Moreover, it wasn't exactly quiet inside the main stable. And from outside came the clang of a hammer and the ring of metal. Gunder, Jens, and a couple of boys he didn't know were busy putting winter shoes on three horses. Calking, it was called.

When Gunder himself was there, nothing much could happen, surely. There was no hurry about getting off for a ride. Svein had just come up to greet the horses and lend a hand today. His pockets were bulging with crusts for Brage and sugar for Flora.

"Hey! It's been a long time." Gunder nodded. And Svein explained about all the composition and sums he had to do at home these days.

But that was certainly not why he hadn't come for several weeks.

The super-horse on the wall had given him no peace. It pierced him with accusing eyes. "You're a coward! Coward! Coward! You don't dare, you don't dare go up there again! What a wretched little coward!"

Well, here he was at last.

Marry! Ugh, girls!

He must have grown a little recently, for surely he hadn't reached as high up toward that hook before?

The harness that had to be polished and greased was unhitched from the wall. He remained on the spot, separating the straps, while he thought about what to say when he went in to the others in the main stable again.

Then something struck him on the head!

"He's killing me!" yelled Svein, and fell on his knees. Gunder and Jens rushed in from one side, Sigrid and Ella from the other.

"Did he hit you on the head?"

Four, six, eight heads met over Svein in a jumble.

"Catch him! Don't let him get away!" Svein managed to gasp.

"Oh, that one won't get away." Gunder was as unruffled as ever while his fingers searched around Svein's head.

"But it's—it's murder nearly!" Svein stammered.

The twisted face above him became even more on the bias. Gunder was *laughing!*

"You've had a bang, all right. Come away and lie down here on the bench." Gunder loosened his scarf and handed it to Sigrid, asking her to wring it out in cold water.

She hurried off, glad of the chance to play nurse.

"Maybe Pronto thought your hair was a wisp of hay," Ella suggested.

"Pronto?" Had Pronto sunk his teeth into his scalp?

Svein looked at the box stall and the head swaying back and forth inside. Yes, he had certainly been standing pretty close to it.

"Did you think it was Rolly?" Jens asked.

As Svein nodded, Jens turned around toward Gunder. "Do you hear that?"

"No. Did you hear him say anything?" Gunder sounded quite amiable and innocent, but Svein realized he and Jens were in disagreement about something. Did Gunder not believe that Rolly had been out to get him the other times?

Sigrid returned with the wet cotton scarf, which she folded together and placed carefully on Svein's head.

"Now it'll certainly get better." She smiled down at him.

Such a fuss! Only a small lump had been raised on his head. Hardly any blood showed on his handkerchief when he dabbed with it.

But Sigrid had soft hands—a little cold, but gentle and kind. They felt quite different from Mother's.

Svein was ordered by Gunder to lie quietly on the bench for a while. Then the men went out again, and it was pretty clear they were carrying on the discussion outside. Jens's voice grew louder than usual, but Gunder's replies remained low and measured.

The girls at last seemed to understand that Svein wanted to be alone. Ella stomped back into the stable, and Sigrid followed reluctantly after her. "Are you *sure* there's nothing more we can do?"

"Yes." He managed to add "Thanks" as they closed the door.

The lump was throbbing a bit. Svein looked reproachfully at the black head that stuck up above the side of the box. The stallion glared defiantly back at him.

It bared its long yellow teeth—the murder weapons! But it didn't whinny. It probably was laughing at him, at the silly little pup!

All at once Svein noticed a challenge in the dark eyes—the very same as he had seen on the wall at home, the come-on-if-you-dare gleam! Pronto was like —it was just as if Svein was looking at the super-horse.

"All right, Pronto, just you wait," muttered Svein. And then he seemed to doze off a little.

It couldn't be possible. No, for it was really quite impossible! Surely it would be just crazy!

The English translation Svein was puzzling over seemed to turn out crazy, too. But when had he heard a thing like that, on his way to school!

He had met Per-Erik and Arthur in the pouring rain. They usually met at the same place each day and kept company for a block or two. Then they could talk about Ligård.

Today they were grumbling because the rain had washed the snow away. There would be nothing but slush in the farmyard, filthy horses, and a good deal of extra work.

"Have you heard that Rolly's come back, by the way?"

"What do you mean, come back?"

"Well, he's begun riding again at Ligård. He's been under 'house arrest' since one day last spring, but now Gunder's allowed him back."

No wonder Svein's translation went all haywire!

A headache lasting several days, a telling-off at school

for badly prepared homework, and now this on top of everything! Just lovely.

He had to go to Ligård and find out if it was true.

The girls, who were washing down the horses' muddy legs, said, "Oh, yes."

And Torkel, who was sweeping muck away into the midden, said, "Yeah."

And Jens, who was walking around like a thunderstorm, said, "Hell."

"Why, oh *why*, has he been allowed to come back now?" Svein asked.

"Because Gunder believes in miracles," replied Jens.

"What do you mean by that?"

"Go ask him yourself."

Gunder was in the buggy shed.

Once again Svein asked, but a little more meekly than before.

"What for? Because he's a *customer*, that's why. He pays!"

"But . . . " Gunder knew better than anyone else all the harm Rolly had done to his horses!

Then Gunder changed. His gray eyes looked seriously and directly at Svein.

"It's not just for the sake of the money. But we'll have to think a bit about you, too."

"About *me!*" Well, now . . .

"It's not to be *dangerous* to ride here!"

What was Gunder getting at?

"When a stallion is wild and pig-headed, there's no use beating him," Gunder went on. A gentle treatment was better, in Gunder's opinion. He tried to get around to their good sides, with both horses and boys. It had perhaps been wrong to chase Rolly away from the stable earlier.

"The horse sense we have sometimes doesn't go far enough. We'll just have to wait and see how things go now!"

Svein saw how they went.

First of all, he saw Rolly in a cowboy outfit with tall, polished boots . . . then Rolly on Blue Boy and Rolly on Brage . . . Rolly doing a show with all sorts of tricks . . . vaulting into the saddle from behind . . . standing in the saddle, riding backward and sideways . . . riding his horse without reins, saddle, or stirrups . . . Rolly being applauded and praised . . . by boys and girls . . . by Ella and—Sigrid!

Rolly, Rolly, Rolly! Rolly the Stinker.

"Hi, Schwein! You didn't turn white, did you, when that guy's scooter came a bit near Brage the other day?" Friendly concern!

"No. But Brage could easily have broken a leg in the ditch!"

"Oh, old Brage had made out before on rough ground. W'd you like to learn how to change gallop?"

"We'll have no gallops in the yard, thanks," said Gunder. "It makes the others over-restless."

Gunder was on the watch all the time: white streak

of hair to be seen in the stable door, at the hayloft, in the shed doorway.

Meanwhile, Jens stamped away muttering curses—away from anything to do with Rolly.

Svein did the same.

The weather had changed once again. It became frosty, but not too cold to take a Sunday ride if one was properly dressed for the weather. And the riders *were* as they sat on the ten horses that stepped out through the gateway and over the crunching frozen puddles on the farm road.

As usual they were a multicolored and merry mixed lot.

Svein was riding with the group. But was he merry? Not very.

The day had begun so well when Gunder said, "You'd better take Sokka today, Svein. She needs a steady rider!"

Everyone knew how nervous Sokka was, and she was in foal. And everyone knew how careful Gunder was about whom he allowed to ride her.

"Oh! Can you manage Sokka?" It was comforting to get a little admiration from Ella while he tightened the girth and fixed the stirrups. Sigrid was busy making friends with Blue Boy.

A lady had gotten Steady, and her husband Flora. They mustn't become too attached to particular horses, Gunder had said before. They would have to change horses very often. "There was to be no bickering and annoyance if you didn't get 'your' horse," ran the stable rule.

No, Flora didn't just belong to Svein. And recently now he'd been going up to Pronto and talking to him. He had treated him to one or two tidbits and tried to make friends with the stallion. It had become his goal now. The day he mastered Pronto, *then* he could ride!

But so far there were only Gunder himself and Jens who could manage that task.

So Svein thought until he saw Rolly coming out of the back room with Pronto tugging and jerking at the reins.

"He's just getting him ready for Gunder," Svein thought hopefully.

But Gunder had to ride Rosemary. She had been ailing for a while with a bad leg and had to be ridden with very special care on this first longish ride. And Jens had a day off. And Pronto needed exercise. It sounded as if Gunder was making excuses. "And you've ridden Pronto before, Rolly!"

"Sure. Lots of times!"

"Aye, maybe you did once or twice. He's got a special bit today, but do your best to be good with him."

Gunder was right over by Pronto. He talked quietly and urgently with Rolly, but Svein had turned away. He felt sick—would vomit soon.

Things got worse when they were all on horseback

and Gunder gave the signal to start. Then Rolly gave another performance.

Pronto experimented a little with leaps and bounds. Rolly sat there glued to the saddle, of course. He forced the stallion backward into place in the line. He backed step by step, with bent neck; he chewed and foamed at the mouth.

The others expressed their admiration for Rolly's skill.

"Now he's pulling Pronto's mouth to pieces! *Now* Gunder'll have to stop him surely," Svein thought.

But no. Gunder merely said that Rolly should ride on and take the lead or there would be fuss and nonsense the whole time.

Gunder himself took up the rear with Rosemary. In that way he could "pick up" all those who fell off, he said.

Svein soon realized that Sokka was quick on the trigger. He was just trying to straighten one trouser leg that had become twisted in his boot. Swish, and there was Sokka at full trot out of line and almost right up to Pronto.

Rolly turned around. "You'll have to take care with that one, kid!"

"Kid," into the bargain! He could take it from Jens, but he could *not* take it from Rolly!

Nevertheless, Svein had to control himself for Sokka's sake, to talk nice and quietly to her, to pat and stroke her. He thought her nerves could be felt through her skin. "Let her trip along for a bit out of line, and then gently and easily guide her into the empty space in front of Farouk once again," he said to himself.

The maneuver went pretty well, but nobody remarked on *that* of course. The new girl riding Farouk smiled slightly, but she couldn't quite be counted.

She sat there proudly and, oh, so ladylike with her riding breeches and narrow-waisted hacking jacket, with lovely high boots and a black riding cap on her head. Mai was her name. Light curls poked from under the rim of her cap.

Sigrid and Ella had scowled at her fine rig. There seemed to be others besides Svein who were displeased with the day's company. But had anyone better reason than he?

Now that Sokka was jogging along with the others as before, he realized how flaming mad to the very marrow he was. If he'd had a lid on top of him, it would have blown off with a bang. As it was, he felt only a thudding and thumping inside his head in time with the slow trot: Death, death, death to Rolly.

Hey! There was Sokka kicking out with her hind legs. Oh, of course, Farouk had pulled her tail. It was his specialty.

"Sorry, I couldn't help it." Mai laughed. "I've held him back from doing it twice already, but this time he was too quick for me!"

Svein steered Sokka out to the side. "I think you should ride out to second-front place," he suggested.

"Farouk respects Pronto—he won't dare to take a chew at *that* tail!"

"Do it, do it, Farouk," he said to himself. "Take a real good bite at it." *There* was the opportunity for an unexpected flight for Rolly, for heaven help whoever sat on Pronto's back when *he* was bitten!

Gunder was eagerly talking horse with the grown-up couple and didn't notice that the ride had altered a little out in front.

For a long way Svein rode all tense with expectation. But what he was hoping for did not happen. Perhaps Farouk *was* afraid of Pronto.

They came out of the built-up area and followed the river for a stretch, in toward the wood. Sokka, more alert than a roe deer, jumped at the least plop in the water and at magpies flying up. *She* should have gotten a pitcher tossed toward her!

"Oh, how magnificent!" cried the lady on Steady. But Svein had no eyes for the frozen fir wood looking like a Christmas decoration, nor for the red winter sun playing up over the icicles on the leafless birches.

He did see how it gleamed, how the bush at the riverbank resembled the diamond pin Aunt Ka was so proud of. But so what?

Rolly was still at the head. Pronto behaved perfectly. Oh, why couldn't he slide here on the edge where it was icy so that the stuck-up puppy slipped off and fell into the river!

People out walking on foot along the forest tracks stopped and waved to the twisting chain of horses and riders. "It looks most enjoyable." Someone laughed. Riders with red cheeks and happy faces waved back. No one noticed that one sat hunched up and unhappy and that he was frothing inside—more than any of the horses' mouths. No one could possibly know.

Suddenly there came a howl from Ella. Little Miss had lain down! She was rolling on her back with all four legs in the air! And Ella, who had toppled off, stood taken aback beside her.

Sokka had no sooner seen this than she, too, began to give at the knees. Svein pulled up but did not dare draw too hard on her. So all he could do was to jump off and away, and there lay Sokka rolling as well.

Rolly naturally had to make something of it. He made wisecracks about sausages and Swiss rolls. Somebody even laughed at his jokes.

"Well, now." Gunder came with a good-natured reminder that it wasn't all that long since Rolly had been complaining about being "near flattened" in the same way. Quite a few of the horses had this bad habit of rolling whenever they came to a meadow with grass or moss that made it tempting.

"But we can just as well have a rest here in the fine sunshine. It'll be grand to stretch our legs. We should have had the coffeepot with us." They never went without it on trips in the summer, Gunder explained.

The brook beside the path was not yet frozen. There was just a little thin ice in the still water at the edges. "Is it all right to give the horses water, Gunder?"

"Certainly," he replied. He thought it would not do

them any harm to have a drink. They were not so warm that they couldn't take a little cold water.

Svein kept well away from Rolly and his court. Of course he was making up to both Sigrid and the new girl, Mai, showing them a place where it was easy for the horses to get down to the water. He had tied up Pronto by himself, for it was no use having him near the mares.

When Sokka had slurped a good deal of water from the brook a little farther up the slope, Svein heard a rustling sound right behind him, and there was Ella pulling her beloved Little Miss. Frozen moss was crushed with a crackling sound under the hoofs.

"We'll have to keep Pronto away from you, you know. He's the stallion." She chattered on about geldings until Svein grew hot about the ears. It was just a short time ago that Jens had explained to him that a gelding wasn't a breed of horse, as he had thought. Svein hadn't known that all the other stallions in the stable were castrated, "clipped" as Jens called it.

He didn't exactly feel that this was something to discuss with Ella and Little Miss, and so he quickly tied Sokka to a tree and made his way a short distance into the wood. He jumped and sprang among the tussocks and eventually managed to run off a little of his anger.

But when he came back to the others, of course Rolly was still standing there with Sigrid and Mai. Then it felt as if the run in the fresh air had been in vain.

"Sigrid doesn't think Rolly is nice. Not *very*, anyway!" There stood Ella again, concerned with what Svein was thinking! He wasn't thinking at all, not what she thought. But there was no point in explaining, so he just snorted contemptuously.

"Do *you* think the new girl is pretty? Mai? She's foolish, I think. She used to ride at the Riding Club. How she can be bothered dressing up like that!"

Now Gunder shouted that they were setting off again. "Come and remount here on the track!"

Mount, yes—but what? Where was *Sokka?*

He had tied her to the tree beside the mossy stone . . .

"Have you seen Sokka, Ella? Can you see her now?" He got a frightened shake of the head in reply.

"Has somebody moved Sokka? Do you know where

she is?" The sound came out cracked, as it does when someone's voice is breaking.

Nobody had moved her. Nobody knew.

"Where did you tie her?" Gunder stood there in front of him—Gunder who had said beforehand that they must tie the horses carefully if they left them. He had also shown them how it should be done, but Svein hadn't looked—he felt too grumpy. He had tossed the reins around a branch and tied some kind of knot.

Svein pointed out the tree behind the clump of bushes where he had dismounted to avoid the sight of Rolly. A dead branch was broken, the very one he had tied the reins to.

No accusing word came from Gunder. He would have heard it, he believed, if a single horse had gone

on up the road. "She must've slipped off quietly for a wee walk in the wood." There were no marks to be seen—none except those that Little Miss had made round about the patches of moss.

"The ladies" were to stay and look after the horses while the men searched afoot. They were also to keep a lookout below the road. But it was not likely that Sokka could have gone that way without someone's seeing her.

The men split into two groups: Gunder with Flora's rider, Torkel and his brother in one direction; Svein, the young rider on Brage, and . . . Rolly in the other.

Although he hadn't spoken about it, Svein sensed that Gunder was anxious about something. And when the order came that each was to go from his own direction toward the steep cliff, the one that descended to the river, then they all understood what it was about.

Sokka could have gone over the edge!

The phrase began to scrub around inside Svein's head—scrub like a horse brush! It hurt.

"Take it easy! She'll look after herself. She's not dumb, Sokka!" It was Rolly who came panting after him.

"She's so jumpy—so edgy. If anything frightens her, she'll bolt—dunno where!"

"Pah! She'll be walking just inside here somewhere."

But she was not to be seen on the meadow they came to, nor on the little bog.

They whistled and shouted, but no nicker, whinny, or neigh came in reply.

Oh, why had he not tied her properly? Why had he gone and left her? He knew it was because he was angry.

Compared with this, what was it merely to have ridden too hard once? You could get more foals—but now it was a matter of both mare and foal.

And the pitcher that time. . . . A short while ago Svein had actually wished that Pronto might take fright and toss Rolly into the river. He had sent Farouk forward with that in mind.

Who was worse? The one running on the other side of the thicket or Svein himself? They would be more or less equal now—equally bad.

Svein could barely find the courage to go up to the edge of the cliff when they reached it and look down upon the river foaming and gurgling over and down the steep slope deep below there.

Still there was no sign or trace of Sokka.

He heard Gunder yelling above the roar of the river. "Go northabout! We'll follow the rapids down to the road!"

"Maybe Gunder thinks she's been carried off by the current? Gone down the rapids?" This suggestion came from the other youngster on Brage.

But Rolly calmed them down once more. "Ugh! The heavy mare could never've run down there. She'd 've stuck like a rock in the river and waved her legs in the air."

Svein had never seen a waving rock before, but Rolly was actually trying to be nice.

If it didn't exactly warm him, at least it took some of the chill off the dread Svein had inside him. He had been frozen as stiff as the moss they were trampling over.

"Where *can* she have gone, then?"

"There's only thick wood all the way in here. It might take days to find a horse that has gone off on its own," the youngster said.

They searched among the tree trunks in the cold, silent wood. If only the snow that had been here before was still lying, they could not have helped finding traces.

Svein became more and more disheartened the deeper they went into the big forest. He noticed that Rolly was going along thoughtfully and kicking roots and stumps with his fine cowboy boots. He was certainly not as confident as he pretended to be.

"We can't risk getting lost ourselves as well!" shouted the third boy when the forest really became dense ahead of them. "We must bear left and get back to the main road."

Rolly sidled up to Svein, who was walking with his head bent. "It's not *your* fault. Gunder shouldn't have let us tie the horses only with the reins. We used to have halters before. They can hurt their mouths with standing and chewing at the bit."

"Gunder can never have thought that anyone would leave his horse—not for longer than it would take to ease oneself."

They had almost gotten right down to the road when they heard it—many voices hallooing and shouting their names.

So they ran once more, and at the bend in the road they met Mai and Sigrid waving their arms. "She's come back!"

It was the loveliest sight Svein had seen for a long time—the young chestnut mare with the white sock on her left hind leg. She stood peaceably munching dead frozen grasses at the side of the road while Ella held her. "She *had* gone down the way—had gone down the hollow all the way to the railway line!"

"The rail . . . " Svein lost his breath and voice once more.

"Don't worry. There wasn't any train. Ella saw a spot where the grass was trampled down and followed the traces."

"Ye-es. *I* was the one who found her," said Ella, beaming. "She *wanted* to come along with me, too."

Svein hung lovingly around Sokka's neck for a good long time, stuffed sugar lumps into her, and told her a lot of things that none of the rest could hear, even though they listened as hard as they could—like Ella.

"Up with you, then," they heard from Gunder. "It's sure been a good long rest we've had here."

"Were you off on a long ride yesterday? You can't sit down now, can you?"

The class teased and laughed and refused to believe Svein when he assured them he was hardly feeling stiff at all.

"I've gotten over all that now."

He soon regretted that he had told them about the trip, though. Several of the boys became disturbingly interested—in *where* he rode, what it cost, if it was fun, and so on. One or two of them wanted to come along and have a look.

"I'm not sure you'd be allowed in. It's pretty full . . . "

Svein couldn't see the need for having anyone else from his class up at Gunder's—none at all.

Fortunately Mr. Storland, their teacher, came with a proposal that made the class forget all about Ligård—though, was it fortunately?

The teacher had some pictures with him of a small hospital for children in—somewhere ending in "garia" or "raria." The hospital was kept up by Norwegian school children, he explained. Many schools made regular contributions. Here at Vold many classes had joined in the scheme.

"Perhaps you'd like to join in, too?"

"Yes!" chorused the whole class.

"Then you'll have to cut out eating sweets, or sacrifice one movie a week, so the money can go to this cause instead."

What sweets and what movie, wondered Svein, when every bit of pocket money went for riding lessons.

"Remember, it must be you yourselves who give it. You mustn't go to your mother or father and ask for the money. The idea is for Norwegian children to help other children who are less well off." A pretty thought! Mr. Storland chewed the thought over and relished it for a bit.

"About how much are we to pay?" one of the class wanted to know.

"It's entirely up to yourselves! One krone, or two or three. It's entirely voluntary. It will depend on how much you get at home and think you can spare. But the more money the hospital gets, the more it can help, obviously."

By and by a thoughtful silence descended on the rows of desks. The teacher surveyed the class and saw some with wrinkled, musing expressions and others nodding enthusiastically.

"Well, think it over. But if we join the scheme, we'll have to agree to contribute roughly the same amount each week. Come to me when you have made up your minds if you want to join and help."

Svein made up his mind very quickly. All his self-earned pocket money had gone to pay for the long trip yesterday. Nothing doing; Svein had no money to contribute.

The very next day some of his classmates reported at the teacher's desk with . . . not only one coin or two . . . but some crackling paper money as well. Mr. Storland smiled and made a note and told them to remember it was *entirely* voluntary.

How beastly! Svein went around biting his nails. His riding was in danger! To get money for both things at home was completely out. And the teacher had insisted, moreover, that they were not to ask mother or father.

At least, so he *said*. But he certainly didn't refuse to accept the contributions that parents "absolutely wanted to pay!" If he had, the amount the class gave the plan would have been a good deal less.

The third day only Svein and a frightened little Miriam, had "forgotten" their money.

When Miriam came along the next day with a dollar, *then* Svein gave up the three dollars that should have gone to his next riding lesson.

Entirely voluntarily . . .

And he would have to bring the same amount each week!

Was the idea that Norwegian children were to do *nothing* but go to school and help other children who lived somewhere that ended in "raria" or "garia"?

Tuba jumped and pranced in the paddock. She threw herself around and kicked in the air with her hind legs.

She was enjoying a break before Gunder put her on a long rope. The lunge, as he called it.

Ella and Sigrid hung over the gate and laughed at the lively young horse.

"Come, Tuba, come," Ella called. "She's not yet half

grown. A teen-ager, sort of thirteen, like you, maybe? Or like Rolly or Mai?"

"Mai's older than Rolly. He's only fourteen, and Mai will soon be fifteen." Sigrid put her right.

"I'm eleven. And Svein is twelve, so the steps go right up. Funny, isn't it?"

"Yes. Look, we won't tell Mama we got hot dogs from Rolly at that snack bar."

"Why not. Oh! Then we'd not be allowed to come here any more. I couldn't see why we should go with him anyway. And the hot dogs weren't good."

Hot dogs! What had they to do with it? The fact was that Sigrid had noticed a helpless expression in Rolly's flat features when he didn't think anyone saw him. And deep down in the scornful, jeering, teasing green eyes there *was* something soft! Then and there her dream hero had ginger hair, wavy at the neck, instead of a fair crew cut.

Besides, this hero was almost as tall as she was. And *that* was most important.

"That Mai's really quite nice, after all." Ella ducked down to avoid the shower of snow Tuba hacked up.

"Do you think so? She's pretty mysterious. Doesn't tell a thing about herself. Can't really expect to be welcomed with open arms, then. Why don't they live any more in the big villa they used to have up there on the hill, for example?"

"Perhaps she's divorcing, too," suggested Ella.

"Oh, no, there's nothing like that. Her father's living in the apartment house with them. Per-Erik saw them moving in. Had *loads* of gorgeous furniture and things, he said. Why doesn't she go on riding in the Riding Club, the snob? Rolly, too, says she's a snob."

Tuba had come over. She stretched her head across the fence once and allowed herself to be clapped and scratched a little by both of them. Thank you—and then she was off on another spree.

"Her coat of hair's so funny." Ella laughed. "Still has a bit of the shaggy foal coat left. It isn't good for the horses, is it, if too many people come to the stable?"

Sigrid looked in astonishment at the little face that was squeezed against the bars in the fence to look after Tuba.

"Why do you ask that?"

"Well, because I said so to the rest of the class. Tone and Gerd wanted to come here with me. They almost *all* want to come cause they hear there's so much fun up here." The problem now was to get rid of friends!

"You shouldn't talk so much about it. I don't say anything at all about what we do outside school. So nobody pesters *me*."

"Huh! You're more like Mai."

That went home! Her cheeks really glowed in the wintry haze. Sigrid decided to try to be nice to Mai, even so. If only she didn't begin to make up to Rolly!

"And Svein doesn't want any others up here either, he said. What's become of him? He missed last time as well!"

Oops! Oh, oh, oh! This would be a blister.

"Have you started sucking your thumb again, baby!"

Svein was busy examining how far the pliers had twisted his left thumb off the straight, so he didn't listen.

Rolly, Kalle, Torkel, and he were busy repairing and cleaning all the sleighs in the buggy shed.

At first he had been rather uneasy about asking Gunder for a job, for Gunder was always kind and let him ride on after time was up. And he wasn't really very much use in the stable in his own opinion.

But then things went smoothly, for Gunder happened to need a good deal of extra help to get all the sleighs in order for the start of the sleighing season.

Svein was certainly a little taken aback when he was shown what to do with an old cutter sleigh, for what popped up behind the blue-painted sleigh beside it but Rolly's ginger mop?

"Are *you* working?"

"Funds are gone—nothing else for it but to sign up for slavery!"

Both Rolly and the others clearly slaved more effectively than Svein. He hadn't done very much in the carpentry line. But it must surely be possible to pull out these rusty nails without flattening each of his fingers.

"Where's your harem today, Svein?" came the question from the blue sleigh.

"Have they got harems here, too, now?" Kalle laughed.

"Not *I*. But Rolly seems to have aimed at one."

"Oh, the Thursday gang, yeah!"

"Right, Torkel. You said it!"

There was a good deal of chuckling and laughter among the sleigh runners. "The Thursday gang" were four healthy housewives who had faithfully turned up for keep-fit rides each week throughout the autumn.

"Sigrid and her little sister were here yesterday," Torkel pointed out. "They were watching Gunder train Tuba."

"Do you know how Tuba got her name, Svein?"

"No."

" 'Cause she made such a fine blowing sound when she farted!"

Now there weren't just chuckles; the whoops were resounding around the room when Gunder came rushing in.

"Jens! Is he here?" He looked pale in the light from the open door.

"No. He went into the stable to feed the horses their oats."

Out went Gunder again. Kalle peered through the dusty little window.

"The police! The car's standing in the yard!"

Slam went the back door. *Somebody* was all steamed up, flashed past sleighs and carts, and was gone.

Rolly!

Three boys looked at one another in bewilderment.

"Who are they really after?" Svein felt a chill down his spine, and then turned hot the moment after.

"Jens. He's the one Gunder asked about."

"Poor old Gunder, he sure looked worried. It must be more than two years since the last time." Torkel laid his hammer down slowly.

"Two years since what?" inquired Svein.

"Don't you know? Jens has had trouble with the cops before—two or three times. Some smuggling business."

Kalle and Torkel wondered if Rolly had shot out to help Jens get away.

It was not very likely. The back door of the buggy shed led into the tool room. From there you just came out onto the fields that descended toward the main road.

The main door creaked open again . . . the sliding door out to the yard.

They were not in uniform, the two men who stood there. They wore ordinary winter coats and hats.

"Hello, is one of you called Rolf Ivar?"

Reluctantly the boys explained where Rolly had gone to. There was no point in denying that he had been there.

The back door had been locked from the outside.

The men went out and around to the back. Someone had gone down the field with big leaps. But the person in question was already over the stone wall at the bottom. There wasn't a living thing to be seen among the bushes along the main road.

"We'd better drive down toward the station and see if we happen to meet him."

At any rate, there was no wild chase with bang-bang and all that. The two of them walked at a normal pace back to the car and exchanged a word or two with Gunder before they got inside.

A black car drove out of a snow-covered farmyard, while three large-eyed faces watched from the shed door. Jens stood outside the stable with the oat bucket in his hand.

"So you thought it was me. But I'll *tell* you, I will, when it's my turn."

Jens turned on his heel and went back in.

Gunder stood alone, a small man in a wide space, bowlegged as usual, but unusually bow-backed.

It was a long time before Svein came back to his normal self again. He had not, of course, fainted, but his head felt so numb—like the day Pronto had sunk his teeth into it.

Rolly—that he could understand all right. Anything might be expected of him—worse things than throwing pitchers or terrifying horses.

But Jens! That didn't figure. Sinister, scowling men carrying crates from ships during dark nights; smooth, well-dressed foreigners with rings and tiepins and diamonds stitched into the lining of their suitcases—such smugglers he had read about and seen on films. But big, easy-going, kind joker-Jens!

Kalle and Torkel had been unwilling to say more about him afterward when it became clear that the police were not interested in Jens. They just said, "Forget it." Decent guys those two, but very different.

Drugs maybe? Yes, *that* seemed likely. All those hashish boys had beards and long hair.

When Svein had rubbed four sets of rusty runners and shafts with a steel-wire brush, it was too dark in the buggy shed to work any longer. The light bulb in the roof had gone out, and so had Gunder, so they couldn't get another.

In the stable doorway stood Mai. She was leaning on the broom and trying to pump Jens. "I heard down the hill the police had been here! Is it true they wanted to arrest Rolly?" she said.

Jens cleared his throat and grunted unwillingly. No, he didn't think so. Pause.

"What was it all about, then?"

"They were just going to ask him about something. And he probably didn't feel like answering. He's most likely got things of his own he'd like to keep to himself, like most people."

Mai nodded and began to sweep.

There was nobody quite like Jens! He who had been so mad at Rolly! And there he stood now, almost defending him. But there was no point in denying anything when the police were asking questions—that much Svein knew. So Rolly would have to come out with what information he had. And then he'd have to pay the price for whatever he'd been mixed up in.

They'd be quit of Rolly once again in the stable for a time. He'd probably go to a reform school, or wherever they sent him.

Was Svein glad about it? Being rid of his bane and the show-off?

He went to the back stable and greeted Pronto. "Now I can get to know you in peace. Without anyone's fussing all the time and telling me what to do and how you're to be handled."

Thank you, but Pronto wasn't going to be handled in any way at all. He cast up his hindquarters and threw his hoofs in the air so that the iron flashed high above the edge of the box.

"We *will* be pals, you and me, one day. No matter what you think, I'll be the boss and ride you as well as Rolly. And it won't be long before I do, either." If only he could earn enough. . . . No, he didn't want to think about money today.

In one way it would feel strange without Rolly around, almost as if—no, not as if the horses were without salt, for they couldn't be without salt.

Svein trotted back down the hill to reach the streetcar. He wondered where the car caught up with Rolly. There weren't many places to make one's escape along the road when all tracks could be seen. Now in the dark it might be possible, but . . .

In town they had already started setting up their Christmas displays in shopwindows. Help, he'd also need money for presents! Money, money, money! Cover your ears—don't think!

Just before Svein turned into his own street, a voice snuffled to him from a dark doorway. A drunkard!

Not until he heard his own name did he stop. He wasn't so very surprised—anything could happen on a day like this.

Rolly stepped out in the light from the streetlamp. He wasn't exactly full to the eyebrows, but a strong smell of drink came from him.

"Here's the one they're after. Just go and tell 'em." He made a grand gesture with his hand, and Svein noticed he wasn't wearing his heavy gloves.

"You'll have to do that yourself. You know very well it's no use trying to hide. What about school? And your folks at home?"

Svein's last remark caused Rolly to laugh so much he had to prop himself up against the lamp post. His cowboy boots were also gone. He stood in a pair of thin black shoes that must certainly have been soaking wet in the sopping snow.

Svein tried to hush the roaring laughter until two gentlemen with briefcases had passed.

"No cops them there. D'ya know wh'r I hid from the cop up there?" He began to laugh again. "I' the tel'phone boot . . . boof . . . blast. Never thought o' looh-look there."

"What have you done, then, that they want to get hold of you?"

"What I've done is to be the son of my father."

"Uh?"

"They got my father day 'fore yes'day. But they haven't hold of his sidekick yet. An' he's the one who'd

133

all the stuff. I know where he is, all right, but I'm damned if I'll squeal. Not a *single* word! Father hasn't told 'em, that's for sure. He never splits on a pal."

It hurt a bit to see how Rolly straightened himself because his father had not blabbed. He had talked quite good sense for a time, but now it became more jabbering.

"There's a lot of everythin' they'd like to know. But they can't make rel-l-latives cough up. Have a slug— c'me on." A half bottle was reached out to Svein. "I swapped it f'r some g-gear."

He splayed his legs and looked down at his thinly shod feet. "Over at a pal's 'long th' lane here. Lot be'er pal'n you, y' lousy snob!"

Snob because Svein had waved the bottle away. It was quite a swap the better pal had made! Gloves and boots for a half bottle.

They stood outside Svein's now. If only all neighbors and acquaintances would stay indoors!

Rolly had taken swigs from a bottle before, no doubt about that. Bottoms up, Adam's apple hopping up and sliding down. "Ahhh!"

"You'd better go home now."

"With the cops standing at th' door with notebook out. Not on y'r life."

"Where has your mother gone, then?"

"Up to one of th' other hags. She doesn't 'xactly sit an' *wait* f'r the cops, either. Anyway, she just blubbers —blubbers an' nips, boo-blubbers an' nips."

"What d'you think you'll do?"

"Go down to the station or th' docks. Join up wi' 'nother bum."

Mother and Father were having supper with Lena and wouldn't be home until late. Mother had said his food would be in the oven.

Before he had time to change his mind, Svein asked, "Will you come in with me? There's no one home."

"Y'r a pal after all." Had Rolly expected it? Hoped, possibly?

"Is it all y'r house?"

"It isn't big. And it's horribly old-fashioned." Svein ran down his home so that the difference wouldn't be too obvious. "We don't even have TV!"

Rolly had. "But they'll soon come 'n take it away." That's what usually happened when his father was put away for a spell and the bills became too many, too big, and too old.

His mother didn't seem to be of much help. Rolly more or less had to look after her.

Svein managed to whisk away the bottle at the same time as the windbreaker was hung up and the wretched shoes exchanged for Svein's slippers.

Before Rolly grew too tired, Svein had gotten a good portion of food into him and a portion of not so good information out of him.

His father had several earlier prison sentences. He had had a regular job all last year, but had met the "sidekick" again in the spring. The first housebreaking job they did together was, as a matter of fact, "th' day 'fore th' day Sokka lost 'er foal."

135

So it *was* Sokka, then. Svein had forgotten to ask about it earlier.

And now in the autumn the latest haul had been made. "Real profeshunal job!" Rolly had gotten plenty of money. "For Dad's not mean whenever he *has* some." How the police had sniffed out who was behind the two successful burglaries was a mystery to Rolly.

Everything seemed less mysterious to Svein now. He understood that it could be difficult to get hold of "decent pals" when everyone knew he had a father who went to jail every so often. No one from school would be seen with him. "Their folks are scared of unfort'nate in-inf . . . infection," Rolly got out after quite a struggle. He was almost asleep.

The older boys he had driven around with on scooters on many a shady mission, they were on the whole just . . . difficult to catch up with, but it might have been one of them "stinkers." Snore.

"Come on, now! You can't sit there any longer. Get up! Yes, we're going upstairs, too. Let's go!"

Rolly cursed and groaned and half hung over Svein all the way up to his room.

Down on the couch in Svein's bedroom with Rolly . . . good night.

Svein wrote a note and left it outside his door: "Have a friend staying for the night." Friend? Well, he couldn't be bothered changing it and finding another word.

He crawled into bed, quite worn out, really. He'd

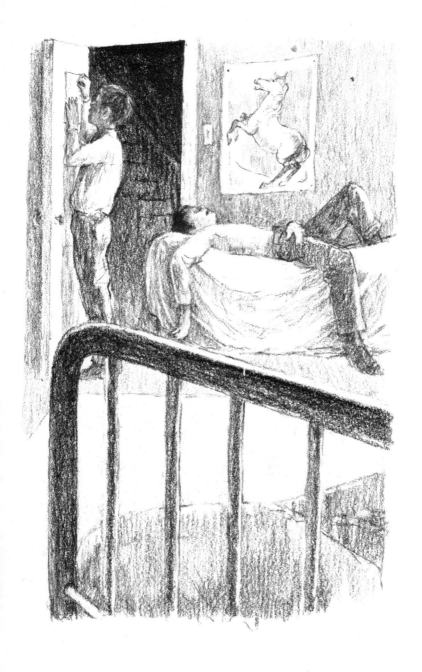

have to try to dash through his homework in the intervals at school.

It was no longer so difficult to understand why Rolly had stuck to his heels for the last half a year.

Svein had known nothing of Rolly's life. And Svein walked alone, now without Finn or anyone to take his place. Svein was younger and smaller, too. Rolly probably needed someone to show off to, as he was the junior in the scooter gang and had nothing to ride himself.

As for liking or not liking, it was quite hopeless trying to figure it out. Svein himself could loathe Rolly or be scared of him. But there Rolly lay, like a ginger-headed challenge, right beneath the super-horse!

And Svein sensed that Rolly needed him, needed him *now* and had needed him the whole time he was banished from the stable. So in some way he was responsible for Rolly.

Quite a new sensation!

"But how delight . . . ful," said Mother.

She had set the breakfast table nicely and was standing with her "welcome to our home" smile. It collapsed as soon as she saw Rolly's untidy appearance, though. Svein and he *had* been together in the bathroom, but not very much good seemed to have come of that.

Father came in rustling the morning paper, well groomed and neat as ever.

Greetings were exchanged, and Rolly was invited to take his place.

It was obvious that the "friend" was supposed to have such a good time that he would want to come back very often, but Rolly did not look as if he were having a good time.

"Do you go to Vold school as well?"

"Naw. Junior High." The spoonful of egg almost slipped out of his mouth halfway through "Junior High," so Mother hastily took her eyes off him.

"Yes, you must certainly be older than Svein. Did you meet each other at Ligård? Are you crazy about horses, too?"

Just a nod and grunt of agreement to Father. A thick slab of butter was smeared on the bread—and the tablecloth.

"Well, in that case I suppose there is some pinching done in your home, too?" Mother laughed.

Rigid, tense silence followed.

"Lumps of sugar and crusts, for instance?"

Neither of the boys laughed.

Mother and Father grew more and more frantic in their efforts to keep up the conversation, and Svein became hot around the ears. With every gulp of milk Rolly took, with every wipe of his hand across his mouth—his napkin lay neatly folded beside the plate—he grew hotter still.

As soon as Rolly had stuffed the last half slice of bread into his mouth, Svein sprang to his feet. "We've got to fly—Rolly has to go home and collect his school gear."

"You live some distance away, I suppose?"

Father's eyebrows shot up when the name of the district made its way through the slice of bread.

Blasted snob! This time it was Svein who thought it.

Out tramped the boys, and "Heaven preserve us!" said Father.

Mother brushed the tablecloth and sighed, remarking that they could very well do without *that* kind of friend. "You should have heard how dreadfully he cursed in the bathroom!"

Cursing was a sign of lack of confidence and a feeling of inferiority, Father said. The more young people cursed and swore, the harder they found it to express themselves in any other way.

"For the rest, I agree with you. *No* more of *that* sort, thank you!"

They had been to the police station the day before yesterday.

Svein had waited outside while Rolly went in and reported that here he was, but he would give no information. There was nothing more they could do inside there, and that was that.

But what had Rolly done with himself today? While Svein sweated and carried buckets of water with both hands, he kept glancing at the door to see if the ginger head would pop into sight above the partition.

They had agreed to go together three times a week up to Ligård. Neither of them could afford the streetcar fare any more.

Today Svein was just in and out of the house long enough to leave his schoolbag, grab some hunks of bread, and change into his ski boots. They were too tight now, but he curled up his toes. No doubt he could go much faster there and back on skis.

But Rolly was not in when Svein rung his doorbell. His mother opened at long last. A fine sight she was, with untidy hair, spotty skirt, and streaming eyes. She didn't snuffle like Rolly when he had been drinking, but she talked as if from the inside of a pan with the lid on.

Didn't know where Rolly was, when he might arrive, anything at all.

"If only he hasn't done something crazy," thought Svein. The police would certainly be keeping an eye on him.

"C'd you hold up this here leg for me, Svein!" Gunder stood with a special knife and was going to cut out the crack in Rosemary's hoof. Always something wrong with her legs.

Svein placed himself with his back to the horse's head and stroked down her foreleg once or twice. "There now, Rose. It's going to be fine as soon as Gunder has fixed your leg."

He was allowed to lift the sore leg. Bend the knee and let it rest on his trousered thigh.

"You'll manage to hold tight while I cut, now." Svein wasn't sure whether it was the interrogative or the imperative grammatical form. But he managed! Even if Rosemary was rather restive during the treatment, her foot was held in place.

Gunder nodded and said he had become a real stable hand, had Svein. And the time had gone quickly, too. It suited him well to have Rolly and Svein in to help now, when Jens was busy with his exams at evening school.

The hoof was carefully smeared with horn salve.

"What's become of Rolly today, then?"

Yes, that was just it.

Svein had soon spotted that Gunder, too, was wondering what Rolly could have been up to. "He must surely have a bit more sense up top, now," he decided. No harm in hoping.

"It's real nice you've become pals, you two." While Svein chewed over how true that might be, Gunder went on to say that there'd always been good friendship in the stable. But Rolly wasn't so easy to get on with; he wouldn't really make friends with anybody, whatever the reason might be.

A gray-eyed twinkle was directed at Svein, but he wasn't the one to hold forth about other people's fathers.

"Oh, well. There's always something. We all have our problems." And then Gunder asked if they had managed to agree about Pronto. Ho! He knew more than he let on, he did.

"Do you think *I'll* be able to ride him soon, Gunder?"

"If you like him and he likes you, well perhaps."

Like/don't like, once again. Was it not enough to feel that a horse was exciting and to have a burning desire to ride it?

The problem was that Pronto still didn't find Svein in the least exciting and certainly didn't want to be ridden by him. He would graciously accept a little tidbit, but when Svein wanted to clap him or talk nicely afterward, then it was bang! and the hind hoofs were hammered into the side of the box so that the woodwork splintered.

Sometimes he peeled back his upper lip and looked plain contemptuous. The silent neighing was something he had started recently. It was rather sinister.

But Gunder said that Pronto was hoarse—he hoped he wouldn't get a throat infection this winter, too.

This time last year Rolly sat a whole night in the stable watching over Pronto. He steamed him with creolin, for his throat was so tight that he was in danger of being throttled.

"The same as false croup?" Svein had had that when he was little.

"Just about, yes." They had taken turns at night, Gunder, Jens, and Rolly. A horse didn't forget things like that. But they had better not hope that Svein would gain Pronto's confidence in *that* way.

"I'll let you try him on the lunge for an hour or so when his throat gets better. Then you can try your strength with him."

Svein had taken a ride on good old Flora and one on Brage. But there wasn't much riding possible with such conditions underfoot, so Gunder said he'd be able to save up for the spring all the hours he was earning now.

"Would your father like you to stop the riding?"

Since the weekly pocket money had stopped, Gunder meant. Svein had explained about the collection in school.

Gunder hawked and munched a straw as he led Rosemary to her stall.

"You'd better tell him about that there arrangement so he knows what's happening! A lot of good is certainly done by those aid programs, though. It's a matter of chance what you hit on. Folk need help everywhere, both those right in front of you and those a good bit away. You'll just have to try and do what you can. So you can dare to look back at yourself in the mirror. You'll need a bit of extra courage to look back when you have a face like this one." Gunder turned up his twisted smile and gave his nose a tweak.

The first sleigh run was booked for Saturday, so he needed all the "old hands" for drivers. "You'd better ask Rolly to come along."

"Don't you need any *new* ones?"

"If they're big and strong enough and have done some sleigh driving, all right."

144

"I'll eat myself big and fat, and I *have* had some trial runs with Jens in the farmyard."

"You can come along with Rolly as a test driver on Saturday, then. It won't be long till you can drive yourself, I'm sure."

Svein knew that Gunder was responsible for the passengers, and he could not object to the decision.

But what about the wild one he felt he himself had the responsibility for? *Where* was Rolly?

Out looking for a job, as it happened.

When Svein came skiing along the edge of the sidewalk, he was hailed from the same doorway as before by Rolly, but without the half bottle.

"Stair-washing every morning from six o'clock!" He'd rake in quite a lot of dough for it, Rolly explained proudly.

"Oh, how mean! And we've lent a hand with *everything!*"

"It's discrimination!"

"Rotten! That's what it is."

"We seem to have gotten some angry young mares in the stable!" Gunder laughed and let down the earflaps of his big winter cap. "Anyway, there's no discrimination against the mares as Kristin and Anne Marie are both going to drive!" These were two almost grown-up girls who had come most faithfully to Ligård and driven sleighs for several winters.

But Sigrid, Ella, Mai, and Guri with the long braids went on fuming about it.

That Saturday afternoon had been livelier than any for a long time around Ligård farm. All the youngsters had turned up and were in full swing.

Outside the boys pushed sleighs into position, beat and shook out skin rugs, and ran to and fro with newly greased reins and gleaming, polished circlets of bells for the harnesses.

The girls had brushed and groomed the horses to perfection and laid the forelock neatly over the front-let, which was adorned with strips of raffia in bright colors.

Every frost nail was examined, so that the horses might walk securely on the slippery ground. Pronto, Tuba, and Rosemary were the only ones that had to stay behind in the stable. All the others were led out, harnessed, and hitched on, the last with some trouble. Many of them refused to budge and would not go into the shafts.

But at last all was ready. And the four girls were not allowed to come along!

"Bit late to come complaining now!" Jens stubbed his cigarette and took up the reins for Blue Boy that Mai handed him. He wasn't *completely* hardhearted toward pleading eyes beneath light curls, was big Jens.

Gunder put some of the damage to rights by saying that the young ladies were naturally welcome to ride in the sleighs as far as town, to the place where the company were to be collected. "Take your seats, ladies. Just choose which sleigh you want!"

Rolly and Svein both followed a slim shape with their eyes. But Sigrid climbed up into Per-Erik's cutter sleigh!

They scarcely noticed that it went "bump" in their own sleigh, but there sat Ella. "I'd rather ride with *you* in spite of Little Miss being so nice! Look!" It was Kristin who stood over there holding the beauty's reins. Mai stuck to Blue Boy and Jens.

"Take it easy, Brage!" Rolly's appeal didn't help much. Brage tossed his head and shook the circlet of bells. He stamped, impatient to get away.

Gunder handed out torches, which were then lighted and placed at the front of the sleighs, and the procession wound its way out of Ligård like a great shining serpent.

Steam arose from the horses' bodies, and the breath puffed like smoke out of their nostrils in the cold. The bells jingled and clashed in rhythm with the beat of the trotting. Their notes were high, higher, and highest in pitch.

How thrilling this was! Svein held up his torch where he stood at the back beside Rolly, who looked like a real coachman with a long whip in his hand.

Ella became quite "ella-ted," as the coachman said. She wriggled with joy in her fur lap rug and clapped her hands. She waved to every dog that leapt aside in panic; to each car and each streetcar as they approached the town.

People came to their windows along the street: small, dark shapes outlined against lighted rectangles.

"Sigrid! Look, there's Mama at the kitchen window!" They waved their arms with all their might, the passengers in Rolly's and Per-Erik's sleighs.

"Sigrid sat with Per-Erik because she doesn't like you two being together all the time now," Ella remarked to Svein and Rolly.

It was probably intended as some sort of comfort to them, this. The drivers pretended not to have heard.

In the square in front of the library all the passengers to be picked up were waiting. They were employees of a firm called Malba that was celebrating its fiftieth anniversary.

They hipped and hurrahed as the first horses' heads and then the whole line of torches came in sight down the Christmas-decorated street. The shouts and ringing bells drew many people to the square to watch the loading.

Now the time had come for the girls to leave both the horses and the coachmen. This didn't take place entirely without complaints, but they couldn't really make a scene either, right under the noses of Gunder's customers.

Three people were shown into Brage's sleigh: one young dandy with his hair sleeked with scented hair oil; a giggling little office girl; and a silver-haired elderly lady in a fur coat.

The boys tucked them into the covering of skins as best they could, and the ladies had brought woolen rugs with them to add to the skins. The dandy refused to be "wrapped up like Glass, With Care!" There were giggles from the little one.

Then Gunder cracked his whip—no one was allowed to use it *on* the horses; only beside them if they were going too slowly.

There was no trouble of that kind with Brage! He set off so eagerly that Rolly had to hold him in. They had to keep a certain distance between the sleighs.

Malba, Ltd., was a jolly firm. Yelling and shouting, screeching and laughing filled the brightly lit Christmas streets and the dark lanes, the wide residential roads as well as the narrow, twisting cart tracks.

Along the very narrow timber track they went, with flying colors.

The trees had thick white pillows on their branches. Hush, hush, whispered the forest. But the silence was split with the shrieks of people and the sound of horses.

Ring-ling, ring-ling, ring-ling. Brage's back moved in a confident and regular rhythm. This was his home ground.

The steam from the horses and kerosene torches warmed them slightly in front, but it soon became cold behind, particularly for the drivers who stood on the frame, with knitted caps down over their eyes and scarves covering their chins.

Even those passengers who were tucked in most snugly got red noses. Or perhaps it was because they had to keep having a slug at the bottle "to keep in the heat." Other things besides woolen rugs had been brought along.

The bareheaded dandy especially needed a drink pretty often to restore himself. He turned up his coat collar and inquired if he might creep under the ladies' furs, "fur example"! The little giggler almost died laughing as she lifted a corner of the rug and took pity on their freezing escort.

"The coachman certainly needs a drop, standing there so exposed!" The silver-haired woman passed a tumbler back. Rolly took it and knocked back a good swig. "None for *you*, though," the lady said jestingly to Svein. "You're too small, my young friend!"

Why didn't she call him "kid" as well? Svein jumped off and flapped his arms to keep warm while he ran along beside the sleigh—flapped both with anger and cold. *Must* she give drinks to Rolly, the stupid, hopeless female!

Rolly got fresher and fresher. He cracked the whip, even though Brage wasn't going further ahead!

Next time the tumbler was passed back, Svein tugged at Rolly's arm. "No! Lay off it, Rolly!"

But Rolly's lopsided grin didn't suggest that he would deny himself anything. He had managed to get a mouthful down when a tall figure overtook their sleigh.

"The drivers aren't allowed to take any alc'hol, Rolly. You know damned well. You stinker!"

"Ugh!" Rolly had his nose down again to the edge of the tumbler, but Jens wrenched it from his hand and emptied it into the deep snow. "Gunder trusts you, fool that he is."

It was certainly a good thing that others shared the responsibility for Rolly, some who were a bit older, too. Svein sighed with relief.

So did Syversen, who was a department head at Malba, when Jens came back to the sleigh at the rear and took the reins again.

The threesome under the skins in Rolly's sleigh hadn't noticed anything of what was going on behind them. It was lively enough in front. But they reaped the benefit of Rolly's swigs shortly afterward.

A little bit further up the hill they had to cross an icy overhang that sloped rather steeply downward. Out in front, Gunder gave his orders, and the others swung over to the side as far as they could to avoid it.

But not Rolly. "Aren't you calked, boy? On with you!" Brage got across the icy stretch even though he slipped a little with bended knees, but the sleigh slid sideways, tipped on one runner, and tilted over, so that the silver-haired lady screamed and the dandy swore.

Svein jumped off and threw his weight against it— Rolly pressed down on the inner side. It righted itself, but only just—only just.

Their trip ended at the tourist hut at Moss Lake. None of the town's big stores could compete with *that* Christmas display. The hut lay shining like a little fairy-tale castle against the big forest. The gleam from

the windows met the torch flames almost halfway across the ice-covered lake.

"How magnificent!"

"The loveliest I've ever seen!"

"Fabulous!"

The drivers sat in the kitchen steam and gulped down scalding-hot pea soup, while their clothes stuck to their bodies. From the big room with the open fire came louder and louder shrieks of laughter to ruder and ruder jokes.

The return journey was long and cold.

When the company had wakened the whole street where they got out upon their return, Svein was more than glad the sleigh ride was over.

Too—festive?

He was pouring with sweat, frightened, tired, and angry.

He had struggled with Pronto for half an hour just to get on his head harness, and hadn't succeeded.

The hoarseness was gone, and Gunder had said that Pronto could now go with the rope if Svein managed to put the bit on himself.

Oh, yes! Svein got him outside and tied the halter to the ring in the stable wall. And then the fun began. Draw his head down and get the bit into his mouth? Not on your life!

Time after time the rope was tugged out of his hands. Pronto was so very, very much stronger.

Then he stuck his nose in the air to add to the fun! Back, rear up, twist about, and lash out! Svein jumped round like a circus clown—waving bit and harness—and skipped aside when hoofs or teeth came dangerously close.

They wre *laughing* at him, Mai and Sigrid in the stable door!

"Let him see a lump or two of sugar! Slip in the snaffle as soon's he opens his jaw!"

Jens could have saved his advice. A whole pocketful of sugar lumps had gone down already. But Pronto had cleverly snatched every lump in a flash and crunched it. After that there wasn't a hope of poking in a finger; the jaws were firmly locked.

"Get hold of his hair, then," came the cry from the door. That was just fine. Svein clung to his forelock and was thrown off as easily as if he'd been a bit of dirt.

"Oh, you stupid mule!"

"He's just playing. You may as well give up. No use fighting with Pronto!"

Svein turned on his heel, marched straight into the stable, and thrust the harness against the wall with a clatter and clash. Ella, when she saw the blazing sweat-streaked face, slipped into Tuba's stall and did not dare open her mouth.

But Jens did, when he had shut Pronto into his box.

"Well done, kid! One nothing for Pronto!" He grinned one moment and gasped the next, for he had received Svein's head right in the midriff.

"Steady on! D'you think you can get the stallion under control when you can't even control yourself!"

And then Jens saw that Svein was about to break down right in front of those gaping girls! That would be too bad.

"Come here, and I'll show you something."

He dragged the boy after him at full speed out of the stable, across the yard, into the servant's quarters, as Gunder called them, and into his room, which lay at the south end of the tenant's house.

"Gunder lives in the two other rooms here on the ground floor. Floor above is rented out to a married couple. Set yourself down—instead of setting yourself at *me!*"

His room was quite a good size and not too untidy. Books were piled high on a white-painted table in front of the window. There was an iron bed with a patchwork counterpane over it and pinups on the wall, a washstand and an electric plate, and some pans on a shelf. Clean, oddly enough. Clothes were hung behind a plastic curtain, and there were some homemade cupboards made of boxes, also with plastic in front. From nails in the wall hung guitar, rucksack, riding crop, and . . .

"It was this here I wanted to show you." The guitar was unhooked; Jens kicked off his rubber boots and used the bed as a sofa.

"I've been paying installments on this for some hundred years. But when I'm mad, I've *got* to have a pling or two to come to myself again."

155

He let his fingers play over the strings. "You should get yourself an instrument!"

Svein jerked so irritably that the basketwork chair creaked. "Don't you start on that one, too. I *won't* play-draw-paint-sing! It's not my line!"

"OK, OK." Jens nodded soothingly and tried a few chords.

"It's just so maddening that I *never* manage anything I've set my mind on doing!"

"You've managed a right good deal, so far . . . a right good deal. You just aim a bit too high, as Gunder says. But that's what we do when we're young and hopeful!" A melody began to take shape on the strings.

"But it's fine to have a carrot like that hanging in front of you. An aim, sort of. You get where you want to go that way."

Jens managed rather more than "a pling or two" on his guitar.

"Have you been playing for long?"

"Well, er, a few years. I tried with a band once. Wasn't good enough, though. Nothing for it but to take the guitar under my arm and come away back up here again. So I know just how you feel. Gunder, too, has an idea of what it's like."

"Are Gunder and you relatives?"

"Relatives! What are they?" The melody ceased. "I was an orphanage boy. Not worth the trouble looking into *my* past. Gunder scooped me up. Brought me here as a stable lad. Asked for grants and loans and things so I could go to night school. Business course. I've finished with it now and have applied for a job. Gunder's so daft he thinks I can hold my own with the others in business! There's something of a carrot for you!"

His teeth disappeared in his beard again as he told about everything Gunder had done for him. Board and lodging free, and pocket money in the bargain, and always something besides. "He's too kind, you know. So kind he'll die of it one day."

Gunder was too kind. Gunder was crazy. Gunder believed in miracles. But maybe Jens *was* just such a miracle?

"S'pose he's paying off his debts, really. The debts he thinks he owes to life."

Svein looked puzzled, and Jens wriggled a bit. "This is not to be broadcast, see. He's to be spared more talk about it."

Gunder had never become the star jockey he had dreamed of being at first. But life was worth living as a trainer, too. He had married and lived in one of the coastal towns, right beside the trotting track. He had also had a little daughter, and it was to her christening they were to have driven that Sunday Gunder's world was crushed against a Chevrolet.

"He had borrowed an old cabriolet and was sitting all dressed up himself on the driving seat and the other two inside. But Gunder was more used to judging the speed of horse legs than car wheels. Before he'd completed his turn into the highway, the American car had cut right through the cabriolet. Wife and child were killed on the spot."

Nothing was said for a time. The guitar was replaced on its nail.

"So there are folk who've had worse problems than how to get up on Pronto's back!"

Jens needn't have said that. Anger and hurt pride had been washed right out of Svein with a shower turned to ice cold. But Jens, too, could listen to something. He might as well appreciate that it wasn't only because he had been self-centered that Svein had been so short-tempered today.

So he told about Rolly, who had come rushing along to the crossroads where Svein stood waiting, earlier today, Rolly with his ginger mop on end, with wild eyes, and *quite* beside himself—breathless.

"I won't go! Be damned if I'll go! Can't I stay with you? Just a day or two, till I've fixed up something!"

His mother and he had been thrown out of their apartment. They had received notice long ago, but his father said that they shouldn't worry too much about *that*. He'd certainly get them somewhere else to live.

As it turned out, he found somewhere else only for himself.

The landlord had had a tough time getting the rent the other times Rolly's father had been in jail, so matters were settled promptly this time. When Rolly came from school today, their things were lying in the street, his mother was with a neighbor, and a call had been made to her relations in the country.

Her brothers were to come with a truck in the afternoon and collect the most essential things. His mother was needed to look after her old father who was ailing, and Rolly was to get himself a job as a farm hand up there, his uncles had said.

But wait and see if Rolly would go to any stinking farm up there—the dump his mother came from!

"But he *can't* stay with us. It just *won't* do! He didn't realize that. He got mad and said *I* could have stayed as long as I liked with him! If it had been the other way round, that is."

"And where is he now, then?"

Svein shook his head. "He raced off again. I don't know what happened to him."

Jens had lit a cigarette. He lay on his bed looking up at the ceiling, following the smoke with his eyes, until he noticed that Svein was sitting rubbing *his* eyes. "Are you cryin'?"

"*No!!* It's just the smoke hurting my eyes."

"Mmh! Puh! I'll stop when I get a job. One of my carrots."

Jens muttered those mysterious words almost under his breath while he thought, for that's surely what he was doing? "Yes, I'll talk to Gunder about Rolly when he comes home from town. Gunder. But you'll have to find out what he's done with himself. Rolly."

Svein tried. He made a detour to the old peeling apartment house in the back street. No one opened the door at Rolly's place, and the nameplate was gone. A penetrating smell of herring filled the stairway.

159

Down by the rubbish bins in the backyard was a collection of various boxes, a stool, a wash bucket, and a huge armchair where two little boys were jumping up and down with great glee. A pile of rubbish had been tipped up and was strewn all over the place.

"Have the people gone who owned this?"

"Yeah! They's moved. They's been throwed out t'day!" Delighted, gummy smiles.

"The big boy—did he go along with them?"

Two pairs of sharp eyes weighed Svein. One of the boys was quite sure that Rolly had been tied up and carried off in a big black car. The other asserted just as eagerly that Rolly had been taken away by the police, for his father had been.

Neither of them had been there at the precise moment of departure.

In the letter box at home Svein found an envelope with his own name on it. Inside lay a key and a note in such an illegible scrawl that he had to stand a long time under the gate light to puzzle out the contents.

As far as he could make out, Rolly's mother had been so upset that he had had to go in the car along with her. But he'd be back like a shot even if he should have to run away. The key was for the outside door of the building where he washed stairs. If Svein could be a good pal and take the job for him for a day or two. Otherwise, Rolly would lose the job and be without money.

The note was carefully hidden, for Svein didn't doubt for a second that if Mother and Father *knew* that he was going out at half-past five in the December dark on a cleaning job, then. . . . No, this had to be done quietly.

Splatter, splash . . . sand and mud . . . squirts on walls . . . clots on mats. Wipe over and sweep into bucket. Splatter, splash. Wring out and dry off.

Poor Rolly. Poor Gunder. Poor Jens. And a little bit poor Svein who had swapped a lovely cozy bed for these thousand—surely—dirty, cold stone steps.

The skin of his hands wrinkled inside his mittens as he ran home.

"Washed stairs!" Mother clasped her hands together. "But my dear child, you can do that at home! And you'll get money for doing it, too!"

"I'm doing it for a friend. For Rolly."

"That person who was here! Worse and worse." Father refused to listen to his claim that he *had* to take a turn tomorrow, too.

"But . . . "

"Not another word!"

"This wasn't quite what I had in mind when I said that he should take up outside interests," Mother complained at the window a moment or two later. She strained her eyes to follow the early bird that dashed out the gate in the dark with his schoolbag dangling. "Heaven knows how he will manage school."

"That is what both heaven and ourselves are going to discover very soon." Father buttoned up his coat. "The report cards will be coming along at Christmas."

A ring came at the door in the evening.

"For you, Svein." Father looked especially displeased, and Svein guessed who was standing there. He racked his brains for new reasons why Rolly couldn't stay there.

But it was an entirely different boy who swung on the porch railing and said "Hi!"

Rolly, all right, but not the hounded animal he had been last time.

He had gotten a lift to town and made his way up to the stable a few hours ago with a borrowed rucksack and a cardboard suitcase rammed full.

"I asked if I could stay some nights in the stable, but Gunder said no." Instead, Rolly was being taken into Gunder's little sitting room and given the sofa as a temporary bed. "Jens has a chance of a room in town from the new year—he *got* the job—and then I'll take over the servant's room, Gunder said." Rolly straightened himself and gave a broad grin. He didn't look as if he was bothered with thoughts of family trouble at the moment.

Gunder, with twisted nose and a shattered life. How

did he have the strength to help others build theirs? He worked in order that he might dare to look at himself in the mirror.

The report card was awful. Svein tried to forget the whole thing until after Christmas, or something. But Father unfortunately had a splendid memory.

There was a big scene—finished with riding, finished with flying out day and night. "Sleigh rides and stair washing!" Father snorted. As if there had been endless numbers of both.

Hereafter Svein could just take things calmly, school and homework.

SCHOOL AND HOMEWORK! SCHOOL AND HOMEWORK!

Then influenza struck Svein seriously, and his eyes streamed, not only because of the cold. He wept not just because of school and homework. He wept for Gunder, for Rolly and his parents, for Jens, for all who were hard up against it, both "those right in front of you and those a bit away."

"Now, now, Svein darling," his mother said when she found him—the same tone Gunder used when he talked to Pronto.

Svein had to turn his back on the super-horse. Not all people could be super-*men*.

For one solitary twelve-year-old it could be too much. So he slept and slept.

Two days before Christmas Eve a ring came at the door again.

Svein was up and about once more but staying indoors.

"It's you they are asking for, Svein." Mother smiled blandly. It wasn't Rolly, then. "The two book girls, I believe."

"What!" Who on earth was it waiting there *now?*

It was just Sigrid and Ella. They told him eagerly, and at the same time, that Gunder was going to give a free sleigh ride to all the children who lived around Ligård. It was traditional. "And we're allowed to come, too, and we're to tell you he needs you to drive! You'll come, won't you? Tomorrow?"

"*Was* it those two who got books from Lena?" Mother wanted to know. Svein uh-huhed assent, and Mother tested the ham to see if it was cooked. "Very nice girls, indeed."

But when Svein began to talk of going on a sleigh ride the next day, protests were plentiful. He was really just out of bed. He could catch cold again and ruin his Christmas. "And you know what Father said!"

But Father was at an office party. Mother was frantically busy. Morten would be coming home the following day. And school was over now, so . . .

"Wrap yourself up well, then. An hour's ride probably won't do much harm."

The Christmas tree was lit in the middle of the farmyard.

But the reflection of the gleaming lights didn't have time to shine for long in the bright eyes of the children. The town children had seen plenty of Christmas trees for weeks now, but not horses! At last the day had come when they might take part themselves in a sleigh ride and not just be content with hanging enviously on the fences watching.

There were wild disputes about sleighs, horses, and drivers.

Gunder's broad sleigh was stormed first. All of them naturally wanted to ride in front. Of the others, the girls looked at the drivers or at the fineness of the sleigh, while the boys eyed the horses. They wanted the liveliest—they seemed to be expecting a real trotting race.

They had to be distributed pretty firmly, those passengers, plumped into the sledges and tucked in, and given orders to sit still.

Svein stood ready with Little Miss's reins and had no doubt about who would be the first to get into *that* sleigh.

"You should come here! Svein's a *very* good driver!" Ella wheedled along two little children who hadn't yet settled down anywhere. "I've made reins like that on a cotton reel," said one. "And my mom put bells on them.

My little brother's getting them for a Christmas present!"

"Room for one more!" Svein shouted when he had arranged these three.

"Take this one!" A little boy was passed over to him from Jens and Mai's overladen long sleigh—a small, well-stuffed sausage with three jerseys.

"Poke your legs under here and pull there!" The veteran Ella showed him how the fur covering should lie.

Giggles and clucks—and then only the tips of four noses showed between the sheepskins and the woolen caps.

"Well, well, you'll *get* one then." None of the little ones was allowed to hold a torch, but Ella was, after all, the oldest on board here. Gunder smiled. "Watch that she doesn't pull over too far to the right and get out of the track! There's something wrong with the one eye. And waken her as soon as she slows down. She's not over fond of the shafts, Little Miss."

"OK, boss." Svein put his mitten to his cap and was fully aware of the admiration with which Ella and the three others looked up at their coachman.

And so the circlets of bells started their dance once more, the whips cracked, and there were waves and shouts for the few mothers who stood patiently, blue with the cold, waiting to see their little ones safely off.

Ella and Svein waved, too, to a pair who swung past with Blue Boy. Rolly had Sigrid beside him. Good, then *he* was happy. And Svein didn't care. He was not coming back here in any case, according to his father.

Oh, but was he not! Could one have an arm or a leg cut off without fighting for it! Stable life had become just as indispensable to Svein after this half year.

"Can't you d'ive my way, p'ease!"

"Drive round by my aunt's house!"

If all the driving instructions were to be obeyed, the procession would have to spread like a fan across the entire landscape. But quite a few of them managed to point out their houses. And torches were waved in front of windows filled with little sisters and doorways with grandpas.

This way he had never gone before. Several times Svein forgot to take care that Little Miss kept on the track, for—*could* one actually live in that tiny hovel, or in *that?* Welfare state, they called it.

But all the children who belonged to this neighborhood sang "Jingle Bells" at the tops of their lungs. And this was *real* joy—so different from the first sleigh ride.

It looked as if the horses enjoyed the song. They pranced as joyously to all the verses of "Here We Go Round" as they did to "Silent Night."

When the procession rounded the wide bend and came out into open country, "The First Noel" rose to the starry skies in the weirdest medley of tones. The beat varied from sleigh to sleigh. Each bump in the road produced a corresponding bump in the verse. The stars might have had good reason to smile down on this band of children. But did they? *Upon* the children, not *at* them, surely.

Gunder stopped when the singers in one sleigh

reached "Then let us all with one accord." One after the other they checked, Svein, too.

Twelve horses stood still. Twelve torches blazed over eager little sleigh travelers. And many times twelve little voices praised God who "hath made heaven and earth."

The few who passed them on the road that evening would not easily forget the experience.

Svein felt that he was part of the circle—a great cord right round the whole earth of children who looked up toward the same heaven and sang more or less the same songs. The earth was not so very wonderful for many of the children. But it could be if the cord held firm!

Ella had crawled up on the backrest and sat holding the reins along with Svein. They discussed Little Miss's eyesight, and whether Farouk, who stood beside her, might teach her to become a crib-biter. The others in the sleigh didn't know about these things, nor were they very interested either.

The run was the right length for the children. They had just begun to shiver a bit, and the container with hot cocoa that Gunder had been keeping warm was emptied in record time. The boys poured it into paper mugs for all the passengers, and then it was time for "Thank you" and "Happy Christmas."

The stable crew assembled to give Christmas oats to their friends, after having unhitched them and removed the harnesses. Pronto received an extra large portion and put up with being scratched beneath his forelock while he ate from Svein's bucket.

"Happy Christmas, Pronto." He would never, never say good-bye! Nor to Flora, Brage, or Sokka either, or Little Miss.

They all had greetings to exchange before they separated.

"Congratulations on the job, Jens!"

"Yeah. They were so crazy, they thought they could use me." The beard was trimmed and the curly hair clipped. Mai, too, thought that Jens had become a Christmas decoration. That even Mai had become a Jens fan was plain to see.

"Well, stable and manger are not *so* full that there's no room for any that wants to come along here on Christmas Eve!" Gunder was pretty sure there would be some drifting along this year, too; some who had nowhere else to go, or who considered the stable the best place.

"Phew! I got a present from Sigrid." Rolly thumped his breast pocket and pulled a face. How silly, his face was meant to say. But it happened to express how proud I am, too.

The next day Rolly had to visit his father first. And then Gunder wanted him to take a trip and see his mother. "He stood me the train ticket. But you'll be along here one of these days?"

Svein hoped so. Hoped! He couldn't bear thinking about anything else! The Christmas greetings were exchanged at speed, and he sprinted through the farm gateway. It couldn't be, simply wouldn't be, the last time!

Not till he started down the hill did he happen to stick his hand in his pocket. There was a little round package with a tag on it: To Svein from Ella.

That the donor's mother came hurrying toward him at that very moment quite escaped his notice.

Nor did Gunder himself recognize at once the young woman in duffel coat and high boots.

But Mrs. Tyrgrend shook his hand and said she must thank him for all he had done for her daughters during these months. "It was particularly welcome because they had a difficult time in the autumn."

Oh, no, the young lady must say no more, for it was *he,* Gunder, who had been lucky and got such "extra good help."

Sigrid had slipped away from Rolly and the other boys and came out with Ella and their mother.

Gunder had received a Christmas hug from each of them, and then the girls and their mother wandered homeward.

"Just think—if only you could marry Gunder, Mama!"

"Now, Ella!" The other two had to smile.

"Then Grandpa wouldn't have to pay *anything* for us. When are we leaving?"

"He's coming to fetch us early tomorrow. They're looking forward so much to seeing us, I was to tell you, both Grandma and he."

"*Must* we go to Bakken between Christmas and New Years when you're working?" Sigrid asked.

"No-oh, no, you could naturally stay with Grandma and Grandpa. But Papa would certainly like to see a bit of you as well."

"Papa ought to come along here, and then he could see Ligård, too!"

Another time, perhaps. But wouldn't it be fun to go along to the Christmas party at the village hall?

Oh yes, a little. And as they talked, they remembered other things that attracted them to Bakken— Queenie's calf, and whether Paul had become any more good-looking yet. And Papa had written that there was lovely ice for skating on the lake.

It might go smoothly, then, this Christmas she had been so much dreading, Mama thought. And the fact that Ella had suggested a marriage with Gunder, rather than that Mama and Papa should move together again, showed that the children realized how inevitable and final the divorce was—and accepted it!

"Imagine—I saw the gleam of your torchlight sleigh ride right down by Li church." Mama's voice was carefree and happy.

"Oh, yes! And d'you know what . . . " So she got the full report of the sleigh run.

"What happy girls are *those!*" thought the lady in the paper stand at Ligård station, as Mama, Ella, and Sigrid came dancing down hand in hand.

ဢ

Svein got such a thump on the back that he lost his breath.

"Hey, you've shot up in the air since last time, brother boy! You're no pigmy any more!"

Morten was tougher than ever, of course. He had invaded Lena's old room with sticks, shin pads, and helmet, for he had to use Christmas for training, see, as he'd been chosen for the school ice hockey team.

What luck that Lena was married, so he didn't have to share the boys' room with Morten any more. These were Svein's welcoming thoughts.

Clip, clip, clip—where was the gummed tape? Mother had given him some money yesterday for carrying coal and some other little jobs he had done for her recently—just something she'd thought up so he could have money to spend. Today, the very forenoon of Christmas Eve, he had raced around the shops and dug out a mini-present for everyone—everyone except Father.

At last he had wrapped up, and written on, the last one. And then, on with his best trousers and blazer.

This was the busiest day of the year, until the church bells began to ring, as they did now!

They did not go to church in the afternoon any more, for Mother couldn't manage to stand. And she said she hadn't time to arrive an hour early to get a seat.

Downstairs there were candles in all the candlesticks. A wonderful smell came from the kitchen, and the table was brightly set.

Lena, Tom, and Mette had arrived and were waiting, decked in their finest, sherry glasses in hand. Not Mette, that is. She sat in her porta-crib and laughed, showing two teeth and trying to eat the pink flowers on her dress. A good thing Svein had bought a rattle for her, so she would have something to occupy her.

The radio broadcast Christmas hymns and coughing in church. Father turned it down and lit the Christmas tree.

"Good health, and Merry Christmas, everyone!"

And then they ate and drank and had a marvelous time.

Behind and through it all, Svein could see the stable. It was like a film where the pictures had been taken on top of one another. Double exposure, they called it.

He saw Gunder and Jens strolling around feeding and chatting with the horses. He saw Pronto's head quite clearly. Or perhaps the head from the wall upstairs?

"Good health and welcome, Tom and Lena. Welcome home, Morten! Good health!" All the glasses were raised.

From the corners they came, out from the shade and the dark, all those who needed Gunder's help tonight. There were many, but none was turned away.

A minister read the Christmas lesson quietly on the radio in the background.

A halo was around Gunder's head. He poured coffee in paper mugs to those sitting on the straw.

Another hymn from the radio, or was it Jens's guitar? He was certainly sitting strumming it somewhere in the stable.

"Let us pray for all who hunger and are in need . . . "

"Can you manage another chop? Just a little one?"

There were three circles in his life. Svein saw them clearly in the light from the candle right in front of his plate. The innermost was home, those who were sitting around the table here. Beyond that were his friends at the stable and others he had gotten to know. And beyond that was the circle from the night before—the one with all the unknown children throughout the whole world.

He himself was a part of all *three* circles. What would he need to be like before he dared to raise the mirror in one of them—or in all three?

Then Morten went around the Christmas tree, handing out the presents.

All were busy with Mette, so Svein was able to open up Ella's little parcel in peace. A measuring tape, the kind that jumped in again when you pressed a knob. Heh! Funny Ella.

He got cross-country skis! And ski boots, rubber ones. And he knew well enough what such things cost, so his folks really were kind. "Lena and Tom and Morten also chipped in for the boots," Father said. Svein went around to them all, then, bowing and thanking them.

Now he could join in the school ski contests without making an absolute fool of himself. And he could get in some training in his runs up and down from . . . ohhh.

"Here comes the flattest parcel of the day! 'To Father from Svein,' " Morten read. He did very well as Santa Claus.

"Another for me. My, oh my!" Father laid his cigar aside and ripped open the envelope with his little finger. "Hm!" He held the photograph at arm's length. "An interesting picture, indeed." This was all he managed in the way of saying thanks.

Svein came over and explained. "It's a children's hospital. And you help toward the running of it."

"*I!*" Father pushed up his glasses and the others craned their necks. "Rubbish. Never even heard of it. Dungas-paria, where on all the earth does that find itself?"

"Somewhere in Africa. I can show you on the map. There are many such places, but *that's* the one our school helps with."

Svein *was* proud. He felt he owned a bit of that bungalow. Each and every one of the little black patients outside was a friend of his.

"Aha, school, yes, I see. I thought you said that *I* did?"

"You've been paying three dollars a week for it for quite a long time. The riding money."

"Aha-so-so-indeed!" Father sprang up, with deep wrinkles on his forehead. But Mother's hand restrained him, her remember-it-is-Christmas hand.

Then Morten continued handing out gifts from the basket.

Before he put out the light at night, Svein nodded good night to the super-horse. It was like an old dream for him now. A smashing dream! But it was no longer a matter of life and death to *own* a horse, nor absolutely to master the most difficult, either.

If, if, if only he would be allowed to carry on going to the stable—to the horses, and to the people.

"It was some trick you played on me there, Svein! I cannot say I like the procedure, either on the school's side or on yours."

Father sat tapping the coffee table with the photograph. Mr. Storland had made copies of it himself as a Christmas greeting to each of the pupils in Svein's class.

"But it *does* all come to the same thing! It's the parents who pay for the others as well—whether they do it directly, or the children hand in the pocket money they have gotten at home!"

"But you were supposed to *ride* for that money. It was for that purpose we felt we wanted to spare it."

"I *have* been riding. Only I paid for the rides by doing jobs. Gunder doesn't give me money, or I could have used it for the collection."

"This is too heavy a load to put on children."

"Yes," Mother chimed in. "If the children really give their own money to the hospital, then they haven't got anything left to use themselves."

"We don't *have* to give so much. But it's great to know about all the fine things the money is being used for . . ."

Mother didn't listen. "That's to say we adults, too, should give a hundred percent of all we have left over."

"Left over from what?" Father inquired sourly.

"These school children really give me a bad conscience."

"Perhaps that's the idea," grumbled Father. "It was much simpler before, Svein, when you raved about things that you yourself understood were not feasible." He straightened himself in his chair. "However, since you have staked so much on it, I am willing to go on paying the three dollars weekly. And I shall try not to think too hard about whether or not I like it."

"For the hospital or the riding?"

"Uh? For the hospital, I suppose."

"Couldn't we rather say you'll go on paying for the riding? And then *I'll* be the one to manage the other thing. Otherwise, you'll have to stop paying, and I'll have to get work somewhere else."

"Steady! You're muddling me up with all this talk!" Father held his forehead to prevent the thoughts from flying away. "The point was that you were to stop gadding about and using up your strength and your homework time!"

"I *will* get down to schoolwork from now on. But I won't manage to read if I can't get to the stable sometimes as well."

"Easy, easy. Nobody can manage *everything*. A systematic schedule is required." Pencil and paper were taken out of the drawer. Father lined off the days and hours of the week. He wasn't an accountant for nothing. Six periods most days at school . . . so and so much time for homework . . .

In the nicely drawn-up squares, room *was* found for "Stable" as well! Twice a week!

"But no late night journeys!"

"No!" Such trips were more suitable for the older coachmen.

Actually it felt quite good having Father straightening things out—more secure, somehow.

Mother had been standing examining the photograph.

"If I go in seriously for dieting—and I should have done so a long time ago—it should be quite possible to take a little from the housekeeping money . . ."

"My cigars," said Father. "It's been on *my* program to cut them out. There could easily be a little to spare . . ."

"For the hospital?"

"No. Let's keep that out of it. For other good causes. We *cannot* let you be so much better than us, you know."

"Carrots are great!" Svein chuckled.

"*What??*"

Oats were good, too. Without them it would never have worked.

Svein had been allowed to give Pronto oats on each visit to the stable ever since Christmas. Finally the stallion became so used to it that he stuck his head out of his box and whinnied for his oats as soon as Svein appeared—just as he did when Gunder himself was in the offing. Nice!

On each new occasion he allowed a little more stroking of his neck and muzzle, scratching of his forehead and under his mane.

They talked to each other, Pronto and Svein. Now and again Pronto was in a bad temper and butted his head or snapped in reply. But more and more frequently Svein got playful dunts and prods, and a neighing laughter livened up their conversation.

Previously Svein hadn't properly detected the difference between dangerous wildness and good-natured frolic—*and* showing off to the mares!

It seemed to be a bit of a surprise both to Pronto and Svein the first time he managed to sneak the snaffle between Pronto's teeth. But the next time there weren't any real protests, either, and soon it was just routine.

Lunging outside, on the other hand, was very difficult.

It was a long time before Svein could stand alone in the ring with the rope in one hand and the long whip in the other, while Pronto circled round with ring and cavesson, as the fine muzzle trappings were called.

"Shout 'trot'!" said Gunder, who was standing outside.

"Trot!" shouted Svein.

"Prr!" blew Pronto and preferred to move at a slower pace.

Then Svein tugged and tried to pull the rope forward.

But Pronto tugged back! The one who fell flat in the farmyard snow and got dragged off was Svein.

Gunder was on the spot at once, stepping on the rope and hauling Pronto in. He showed Svein the reserve slack he should have let out on the rope when he was in trouble. Try again.

Svein managed to make most of the possible mistakes: showed Pronto the whip when he should *not* have seen it, and forgot to let him feel the whiplash against hindquarters or withers when *that* was the thing to do.

But *one* day it went really well. Pronto trotted round the ring as obedient as a well-trained gelding, but so much more grandly! Svein got him both to slacken his pace and increase it to a little gallop.

"That's fine. He's run the worst off himself. You can put the saddle on him now," Gunder said.

Saddle Pronto!

The sun shone. It was a day at the end of February, a day of sparkling sunshine.

The day!

Gunder held the stallion while Svein put on the saddle—while he just managed to heave it up on the tall back, to be more accurate.

Off with the cavesson and on with the ordinary bridle. Gunder helped. He himself used a curb bit on Pronto, but this would have to do. A few firm words in Pronto's ear, and then the usual:

"You can get up, now."

Svein couldn't manage any elegant Rolly-leap from behind, but he got into the saddle under his own steam, after having bribed Pronto with some lumps of sugar.

This was a horse to be on, for sure!

The same restlessness in the veins as Sokka, felt Svein, only so much more powerful in every reaction.

"Talk a little to him. He knows the language!"

"There, there, Pronto, you will let me sit on you, won't you?" Clap and stroke while he tried to see if he wanted to.

Dance steps and little bounds, his muscles tensed and relaxed. Ears flipped back and forward at first, but then gradually straightened themselves up nicely.

Then Svein allowed his body to take over the talking and tried cautiously.

And they were still on talking terms, Pronto and he! He allowed himself to be guided by reins, heels, and legs: turn—press—relax.

Then into the ring track they went. Head up! Most super-horse in the world!

Carrot tasted divine!

Svein would have liked to sing "Glory hallelujah" as he trotted around the farmyard in the brilliant sunshiny weather with glittering drops falling from all the trees. But it would have been unwise to take anything for granted. Pronto could very quickly upset his position in the league.

They applauded Svein from the stable wall—Rolly, Sigrid, and Kalle. And Ella stood jumping up and down in her eagerness, her hand in Gunder's.

"Congratulations," said Gunder with a smile. And *those* congratulations were genuinely meant. "It was a good job you managed Pronto before we sell him."

Sell Pronto? Svein nearly fell off the horse's back. He'd heard wrongly, surely?

No. Correctly. Gunder hadn't wanted to talk about it before. He'd hoped that Svein would first manage what he had struggled so hard to achieve. But it had certainly been touch and go, for today was the last chance. The purchaser who was interested in Pronto was expected at any moment.

Svein was speechless.

"I can't have any stallion in the stable, see." It just caused trouble and made difficulties. And Svein surely wanted Pronto to remain the lad he was? "He shouldn't become any gelding, now, should he?"

"No-o-o."

He got the stallion cheaply about a year ago, Gunder said, because Pronto had been so stupidly handled that nobody believed he could ever be well behaved again. But he was now so good that anyone at all could cope with him.

"Thank you," said Svein.

Now there was a good hope of *making* a little by selling Pronto, and *that* would come in very handy. Gunder talked away at a remarkable pace. He seemed to be afraid that Svein might take it too hard.

"That's what life's like, son," he said as they went together into Pronto's box with him. "It's a real queer mixture of good and bad, black and white. You just have to take it as it comes and keep on going if you are to get anything done. It doesn't last all that long."

Svein couldn't say whether the last was a consolation or a complaint. But Gunder, who was speaking so fast from sheer embarrassment, mustn't be allowed to think that Svein was broken-hearted because of it all— Gunder who had himself known so much bad and black.

"One must get used to changes in the halters now and then—you've said that yourself before." Svein thought of Flora, his first love. And he managed to smile!

The wrinkles on Gunder's forehead flattened with relief. He rolled toward the door, assuring Svein, "He's an experienced breeder and a first-class horseman, what's goin' to get him!"

"Sure, he wouldn't let 'em go to another hoodlum, of course!" It was Rolly who now stood in the back room beside Svein. "D'you know that Pronto's the father of the foal Sokka's going to have?"

No. Even more news.

"Be interesting to see what it'll look like, and if it's a stallion or a mare! And we'll soon be riding Tuba—guess if that'll be a show!" Rolly was bucking him up for all he was worth. Decent.

"Come on over and see what my place is like, will you?"

The servant's room had been Rolly's for some weeks already, but changes were constantly being made, for he was clever with his hands, carpentering and doing things up. Gunder thought carpentry work would just suit Rolly.

He ought to start his apprenticeship somewhere when he finished with Junior High in the spring and then try to get into a vocational school. And if Gunder had said that much, he would be sure to see that it was carried through, too.

"Gunder seems to think it's OK for me to stay here." Rolly let Svein have a trial sit in the repaired armchair. "It was empty after Jens left, you know."

"Sure! But do you manage to still wash stairs before school begins when you've so far to go?"

"Nope, he didn't want me to carry on with that job. But it isn't *enough*, that grant or allowance, or whatever it's called that my mother gets. So I'll just have to give arsenic to the woman that washes the main building at Ligård! Then I'll get her job and add to the payments."

Svein had rather a bad conscience because he him-self was spared the sort of problems Rolly struggled with. In return he complained about how closely they watched over him at home, with his homework.

"Huh! Gunder's a good one, too. Sits on top of me, he does, at night!"

Not a bad thing, perhaps. Then Rolly couldn't fly out and meet his cronies.

They strolled back to the yard again.

"How's Jens these days?" inquired Rolly, for Mai came through the gateway at that moment.

She laughed. "He's got quite good lodgings but a fu-rious landlady! She blows her top if she sees a girl! In his room, I mean."

Moreover, Mai was busy "polishing" Jens. "He *can* behave well and talk nicely, if he wants to," she said. "But up here he wants to be himself."

"Maybe he'll brush and groom some of the polish off you in return." Rolly grinned. "It's needed!"

Apart from the hair-and-beard trim, Jens was just "the same ole villain," Rolly assured them. But all seemed to be going well with the job.

Kalle tightened the girth and adjusted the stirrup leather for Sigrid, who was to have a go on Farouk today. At the moment Sigrid was enjoying a change both of horses and admirers. But Rolly didn't look as if it were the end of him. He had enough to occupy him, with the entire responsibility for the stable when Gun-der was away.

"You'll have to talk to Rolly there," said Kalle, nodding to a new arrival, a boy around Ella's age.

"Uh, huh. You'd better come in and meet the horses, then." Rolly squared his shoulders and strode manfully in front of him into the stable.

"Meet Little Miss, *I'll* bet." Ella was a bit offended, but she, too, had had to get used to giving way to others.

A big girl! He wasn't the only one who had stretched out during the winter, Svein noticed.

Drip, drip, from the icicles over the stable door.

"At Easter we're going to our hut with Papa," said Ella. "But in the summer, *then* we'll be going on a horse trek to the mountains, a real long trip, you know. Can't you come, too, Svein?"

"Doesn't it cost an awful lot?"

"Yes, several hundred kroner, I think. But if we get a little from Grandpa and a little from Papa—he thinks it's fun that we go riding—then Mama will pay the rest. She'll save on our food while we're away. You can say *that* as well. Try, anyway?"

Ella looked disappointed that he wasn't going home with them, but Svein, of course, had his skis.

He made a quick change from rubber boots to ski boots, slung his rucksack on his back, adjusted his bindings, and waved his ski stick at Ella. "See you, then! So long!"

Then he thrust his way down the slope, straight down the gleaming white fields.

Summer trip—a new, tempting carrot dangling in front of him there?

It was hard to say. There seemed to be plenty of carrots—in all the circles!

DATE DUE